Shannon smiled at Gary.

"I've had this here before. It's the best I've ever had." She turned back to Todd. "There's one at the bookstore that runs a close second, though."

Gary continued to look solely at Shannon, ignoring Todd. "That may be so. But nothing beats pure chocolate. Like, for example, a chocolate kiss."

Shannon dropped her fork.

Todd nearly choked at Gary's mention of a chocolate kiss. He'd wondered if Gary had seen the note with the kiss attached the day he went into Shannon's drawer. Now, after hearing his roundabout reference to it, he knew he had.

Gary smiled and leaned slightly closer to Shannon. "I love chocolate, too."

Todd's stomach took a nosedive into his shoes. Unless he was mistaken, Gary had just intimated he was somehow connected to the chocolate kisses Todd had been leaving for Shannon every day.

Todd cleared his throat, hoping his voice would come out sounding casual. "I think most people like chocolate, Gary."

Gary's expression turned smug as he watched Shannon take a shaky sip of her coffee. "Probably. Just some people think chocolate is more special than others. Sometimes it even carries a message."

GAIL SATTLER lives in Vancouver, B.C. (where you don't have to shovel rain) with her husband, three sons, two dogs, five lizards, and countless fish, many of whom have names. She writes inspirational romance because she loves happily-ever-afters and believes God has a place in that happy ending. Visit Gail's Web site at www.gailsattler.com.

Books by Gail Sattler

HEARTSONG PRESENTS
HP269—Walking the Dog
HP306—Piano Lessons
HP325—Gone Camping
HP358—At Arm's Length
HP385—On the Road Again
HP397—My Name Is Mike
HP406—Almost Twins
HP433—A Few Flowers
HP445—McMillian's Matchmakers
HP464—The Train Stops Here
HP473—The Wedding's On
HP509—His Christmas Angel
HP530—Joe's Diner
HP554—A Donut A Day

Don't miss out on any of our super romances. Write to us at the following address for information on our newest releases and club information.

Heartsong Presents Readers' Service
PO Box 721
Uhrichsville, OH 44683

Or check out our Web site at www.heartsongpresents.com

Secret Admirer

Gail Sattler

Heartsong Presents

A note from the Author:

*I love to hear from my readers! You may correspond with me
by writing:*

> **Gail Sattler**
> **Author Relations**
> **PO Box 719**
> **Uhrichsville, OH 44683**

ISBN 1-59310-096-5

SECRET ADMIRER

*Our mission is to publish and distribute inspirational products offering
exceptional value and biblical encouragement to the masses.*

one

"Shannon, I'd like you to meet the new dispatcher, Todd Sanders. Todd, this is Shannon Andrews, our payroll clerk."

Shannon squeezed her eyes shut at the sound of the name. It couldn't be. It just couldn't.

"Hey, Shan-nooze. Long time no see."

That voice. The hated nickname. It could be, and it was.

"Todd," she muttered. "Long time no see." Shannon forced her eyes open and gave him a welcoming smile, even though it was almost painful. She wanted to pinch herself to wake up but knew it wouldn't help her present nightmare. Gary, the operations manager, smiled first at her then at Todd. "You two know each other? It's a small world, isn't it? Come on, Todd. I'll introduce you to the rest of the staff, then we'll get you set up at your station."

All thoughts of the coming payroll deadline deserted Shannon as she watched Gary introduce Todd around the office. She hadn't seen Todd for a long time, and it was no loss. Briefly she considered turning in her resignation, then banished the thought. She would be strong and show him he no longer affected her.

Unpleasant memories flashed through her mind. From the time she was eight, Todd and her eleven-year-old brother Craig had been best friends. The day she moved out was the day she finally stopped having to bear the brunt of Todd's teasing.

During the time leading up to her high school graduation, she'd foolishly thought she was in love with Todd. However, the painful, constant jabs about being nothing more than his friend's bratty kid sister cured her. Thankfully, she got over

5

her high school crush before he discovered how she felt. If he had, she never would have lived it down.

Over the past two years, Shannon had avoided Todd, seeing him only when Craig dragged him to one of their church functions. Despite the safe atmosphere of the church she'd grown up in, those occasions always affected her, bringing back the memories of past hurts, even after all that time. Fortunately, it didn't happen often. In the past year she hadn't seen him at all. Maybe that was why seeing him now at work, it hit her with a double whammy.

She thought she had put Todd and his idiocy behind her. Obviously, she was wrong.

Shannon forced herself to return her attention to her work. She'd almost completed the warehouse payroll when she felt someone poking her arm.

"Shan! I'm talking to you! Have you met that new dispatcher? He sure is a sweetheart, isn't he? Wouldn't you love to meet him in a dark corner one night?"

In the light or dark, despite his good looks and charming ways, which he used when it suited him, she'd already seen enough of Todd Sanders to last a lifetime. "No," she muttered through gritted teeth. The last time she met Todd in a dark corner she hadn't known he was there until too late. That time, he had scared her half to death with some furry monster toy. She didn't hear the end of it for months.

Without fail, every time she went to her parents' home for a family occasion, her brother regaled her with never-ending tales of Todd that she didn't want to hear. According to Craig, Todd had turned his life over to Christ about a year ago. He claimed Todd had changed and grown up a lot since then. Regardless, even though his faith would make a lot of changes in him, deep down, Shannon knew he was still the same old Todd. She was sick to death of his immature pranks. Out of self-preservation, she intended to avoid him as much as possible.

"Hey, Shan. Aren't you coming for lunch?"

Shannon shook her head. "No. I'm going to work through my break and catch up on a few things. I have a three o'clock cutoff deadline on this, and it's going to be close."

❧

Todd walked into the lunchroom, but Shannon wasn't there, leaving him strangely disappointed. He'd always enjoyed their verbal banter over the years. Even though the sharp repartee didn't belong in the work environment, that didn't mean they couldn't talk civilly to each other during break time.

He hadn't seen much of Shannon since she'd moved into her own apartment. In fact, the last time was probably at least a year ago. He thought of her often, and seeing her now only emphasized how much he'd missed her. Todd found it amusing that she hadn't noticed him when he came in to apply for the job, but he'd seen her. At the time, she'd been concentrating on the computer screen at her desk, oblivious to all else around her. Either she had grown prettier in the last year, or the old saying about absence making the heart grow fonder was true after all.

He'd liked Shannon for years. Since she was his best friend's kid sister, though, he didn't want to damage his friendship with Craig. Most of all, he didn't want to get beaten to a pulp if any relationship between them went sour. He'd done whatever he had to in order to keep everything the same as it had always been, maintaining a safe emotional distance. Sometimes, he'd even deliberately done things to push her away, rather than risk getting too close.

Gary and one of the other dispatchers joined him at the table, spread their lunches out in front of them, and began to talk about the events of the day. Todd responded to a few comments, but his thoughts kept drifting back to Shannon.

He remembered the crush she'd had on him when she was in high school. He'd never been so flattered in his life. But, while Shannon had graduated with honors, he'd been working two jobs to pay off a major debt not of his own making. Plus, he'd been going through a rough time at home with his mother, which had become increasingly worse since his father left. Instead of dealing with his problems, he'd taken out most of his frustrations on Shannon, over and above the usual jokes he played on her as Craig's kid sister. She hadn't deserved it. Memories of his behavior still filled him with guilt, even after all this time.

In hindsight he realized life would have been easier if he'd shared his troubles with Craig sooner, but he'd been too proud and too overwhelmed to ask for help.

But that was years ago. Todd pushed a past he couldn't change to the back of his mind and concentrated on things as they were today. Over the years, Shannon had grown from an awkward, mouthy kid into a witty, attractive woman. Todd tried not to smile as he thought of his last view of Shannon, typing away at her computer. He'd always teased her about being nerdy with her aptitude for figures; he hadn't wanted to admit how proud of her he'd been since mathematics was never his strong suit.

Now, after much hard work, at the young age of twenty-five, Shannon had become the chief payroll administrator for a multinational courier corporation. Through Craig, Todd knew the extent and responsibilities of her job, and it bothered him that Gary had referred to her as only a clerk. She deserved more respect than that.

He couldn't erase the past, but Todd figured that since they would now be working together, it would be a good time to make a new future. Her graciousness in the face of defeat had always impressed him. Even though she didn't know it, she'd always held a piece of his heart in the palm of her hand.

The timing may not have been right to start a relationship with Shannon Andrews before this, but things were about to change. He hadn't been a Christian long in the overall scheme of life, but he didn't think it a coincidence that God had placed him at Kwiki Kouriers for a good reason; he felt sure that reason was Shannon.

First he'd catch up on old times and tell her all that had changed in the last year or so. He imagined the two of them, walking down the beach, barefoot, hand in hand, the water lapping around their ankles as they talked. Of course, it would be different without Craig present. Todd couldn't remember ever being alone with Shannon for more than a few minutes at a time. That, too, was about to change.

Since the beach wasn't very realistic, Todd thought of other places to be alone with Shannon and where the best spot for that kind of conversation would be. He imagined them sitting side-by-side in a dimly lit restaurant, romantic music playing in the background, where they could have a special quiet time, just the two of them.

Todd shook his head. They were nowhere near that stage in their relationship. The most likely place for them to spend time together without the encumbrance of work would be after church on Sunday morning, although he didn't want to wait a week just to talk. He'd been attending Craig's church recently, and he missed not seeing Shannon there. Craig had told him Shannon now attended a small church close to her apartment, along with some of her friends who lived nearby. She attended church with her family only when something special was going on. However, those occasions seemed to be when Todd was unable to attend. It was almost as if she planned it that way.

Todd frowned as he checked his watch. The lunch break was nearly up, and Shannon still had not appeared. He wanted to detour past her desk to talk but decided against it since it was his first day at the new job. Instead, he would leave it up to her to approach him.

She didn't approach him all week. She worked through her lunch every day, and he heard talk that the rest of the staff was starting to wonder why she suddenly had so much extra work to do. He had a nagging suspicion her work wasn't the reason for her absence at lunchtime—he was.

By Friday, Todd couldn't stand it any longer. He didn't want to risk a confrontation in the middle of the office, so at the end of the day when he left the building, he didn't leave the parking lot. He leaned against the fender of her car, crossed his arms, and waited.

He didn't wait long. Soon Shannon rushed out the back door at a near run, straight for her car, and straight for him.

Her feet froze on the spot as soon as she saw him. "What are you doing here?"

"I've wanted to talk to you all week, but you seem to be avoiding me."

"Me?" She laughed a very humorless laugh. "Why would *I* avoid *you?*"

Todd covered his heart with his hands. "I detect a hint of sarcasm in your voice, Shannon. If I were the sensitive type, which I am, by the way, you could hurt my feelings."

She snorted. "Move over, Todd. I have places to go. I don't want to run you over, but I will if I have to."

"The only thing you've run over is my poor heart."

She snorted again. "Give me a break."

"Come on, Shannon. Seriously. I think we should go somewhere and talk. We can go out for supper. I'll even pay."

Rather than the enthusiastic response Todd would have preferred to see, she stared at him in open astonishment. He couldn't help but feel stung.

"Is this some kind of joke? You wouldn't take me to some place that serves frog legs, would you?"

"Frog legs?" He watched her cross her arms and tap her foot while his mind raced, trying to figure out the significance of her remark. "Oh! Frog legs! That was just a joke!"

She wagged her finger in the air at him, then stabbed him in the chest with it. "I have never been so embarrassed in my life. Imagine when I got to work, opened my lunch bag, reached in for my sandwich and touched a cold, slimy frog instead! When I screamed and nearly fainted, they were ready to call either the funny farm or an ambulance."

"You mean you didn't look in the bag before you left the house? You took the frog to work? It was my idea, but it was Craig who took out your sandwich and put in the frog before you left."

Instead of replying, she lifted her purse. Todd ducked and raised his hands to protect himself, but she wound back and whacked him anyway.

"Not only did I take the frog to work, but it took my entire lunch break to drive around and find a park with a running stream so I could let the poor thing go. No pet store would take it, and I couldn't wet it with chlorinated tap water! And then I had to face everyone's jokes for weeks."

"I'm sorry. I really am."

"Get out of my way. I'm going home. Alone."

Dazed, Todd stepped aside and watched as Shannon jabbed the key into the lock. She swung the door open, hopped in, slammed the door, and took off with a squeal of rubber.

The woman used up her entire lunch break to save a frog he'd found in a ditch? Todd was suddenly hit by what he should have realized years ago. He was in love with his best friend's sister.

Todd frowned as her taillights disappeared around the corner. Over the years, he'd been less than kind to her, but in the end, she always forgave him, which he now saw made him love her even more. This time, however, it looked as if he'd gone too far. He recalled that not long after he convinced Craig to put the frog in her lunch bag she moved away from home. The Bible spoke of forgiving someone seventy times seven, but the frog might have made seventy times seven plus one.

It would be the hardest thing he'd ever had to do, but he had to show Shannon how sorry he was—and somehow convince her to take him seriously as her Mr. Right for the rest of her life.

He knew she didn't like frogs, but he knew her well enough to know what she did like.

All he had to do was figure out what to do about it.

two

Shannon ran from her parking space into the office then stiffened in an effort to appear dignified as she walked to her desk, past everyone else who was already hard at work. In four years, she'd never been late, until today. All night, she'd tossed and turned and hadn't fallen asleep until almost dawn. Then she slept through her alarm.

It was Todd's fault.

On Friday night, she thought she made it clear when she told him to leave her alone, but as usual he didn't listen. On Sunday morning, she'd gone to church with her family to see her brother sing a solo, and Todd had arrived. When she realized he was going to sit beside her, Shannon moved to the end of the row. Todd had never been one to take hints. To her dismay he sat beside her again. To show him she had no intention of being near him and that she wouldn't let him manipulate her, she moved again. She squeezed herself between her parents, which she hadn't done since she was five years old. Both of them had been shocked but said nothing at her childish behavior.

Todd had driven her to it.

She busied herself in her work, then nearly snapped her pencil in half at the sound of a familiar, deep male voice beside her.

"Good morning, Shannon."

She refused to look up. She began adding a row of figures, pushing the keys on her calculator much harder than necessary. "Good morning, Todd."

"Ah. You said good morning rather than grunting at me. I'm making progress."

13

Shannon hit *total,* clasped her hands on the desk in front of her, and turned her head to look up at him. "May I help you with something, or are you here just to torture me?"

At her words, he sighed, his playful grin dropped, and he rammed his hands into his pockets. If she didn't know him so well, she might have felt guilty for bruising his feelings. Even when he didn't try, Todd exuded a unique charm. Fortunately, she was immune. After one agonizing week, though, at least half the female staff was infatuated with him. His sparkling brown eyes were exactly the same color as his hair, except in the peak of summer, when the sun bleached it almost blond. People always counted on him to liven up any situation, which he always did. Except for when she bore the brunt of it, which was most of the time, Shannon hated to admit she also enjoyed his sense of humor.

"All I wanted to do was ask if you would be as busy this week as you were last and if you were going to start taking your lunch break again."

She couldn't lie. She expected he would eventually figure out she was avoiding him. This week she refused to play mind games with herself. If Todd was in the lunchroom at the same time, it didn't matter. He wasn't going to stop her from eating. She refused to give him control of her life or let him intimidate her anymore. "I'll be taking my lunch break at the regular time."

His grin returned, and his brown eyes lit up. Eyes a woman could get lost in. Shannon forced herself to remember this was Todd Sanders.

He leaned forward and covered her hands with one of his. "Would you give me the honor of sitting with me?"

Shannon yanked her hands away. "Never."

He snapped his fingers. "Can't blame a guy for trying."

Why he wanted to sit with her, she would never know. A week had passed, and everything was normal except for the constant reminders of his presence. Shannon wondered if perhaps she might have misjudged him by expecting that he would still play foolish pranks or bring up embarrassing moments in front of their workmates. But just because he was behaving himself at work didn't mean she could trust him to be the same when they were alone. Even if she could eventually trust him, that didn't mean she wanted to spend her breaks with him.

Over the weekend, she'd spent much time in prayer, trying to convince herself to forgive and forget. When she'd done the same over the years he had disappointed her again and again. After his little performance Sunday morning, Shannon decided to err on the side of caution.

"If you'll excuse me, I have work to do." She picked up her pencil and continued with her calculations.

❧

Todd returned to his station. He tried to be happy but couldn't. He still felt guilty knowing she had avoided going into the lunchroom the previous week because of him. It gave him some relief to know she had progressed to sitting voluntarily in the same room with him. But Todd wanted more.

He wanted to sit at the same table with her and start fresh. He wanted her to like the new, slightly improved Todd Sanders.

It had been over a year since he'd left the old Todd behind. At the time, he'd had a serious heart-to-heart talk with Craig, and in that one day, his life changed forever. Craig had always been a steadying influence, especially throughout the years leading up to his parents' divorce. While growing up, he spent more time at Craig's house than his own. There he'd seen the way a normal family lived, compared to the constant fighting, bickering, and even violence he was used to.

Craig had taken him to his church's youth group meetings a number of times and talked to him often about the love of Jesus, but Todd had always shrugged it off, not feeling very lovable. Then one day, when he was talking to Craig, years after he'd become an adult and stopped going to youth group, something inside him snapped. He thought he'd been handling things just fine, but suddenly, everything came spilling out. He surrendered control of his life to Jesus, and in finding Jesus he found himself.

It was time to move forward and correct some past mistakes, and Shannon was one of them. Not just one—Shannon was the most important.

He watched from a distance until Shannon was settled in the lunchroom with her lunch spread in front of her so she couldn't move then to another table without looking odd to her friends. Todd sucked in a deep breath and gathered his courage. He cleared his throat, marched to her table, and sat in the empty chair beside her.

"Hi, Shannon. Mind if I join you?"

She nearly choked on her food, but he pretended not to notice.

He wanted to slide his chair closer to hers, but everyone else at the table, all women, was staring. He gave them his best smile, then winked at the youngest, whom he recognized as the file clerk. She giggled, making him wish a certain someone else would be as enthusiastic about his presence.

"Yes, Todd? Did you forget to turn in some of the drivers' time cards?"

He pretended to shiver at her cold response, knowing she would pick up his meaning from past experience, but none of the other women would.

She had the grace to blush.

He plunked his lunch tote on the tabletop and proceeded to empty the contents. The women stared as he pulled out the individual containers one at a time, moving aside their own lunches to make room on the table.

"You're going to eat all that? Well, some things never change."

Todd patted his flat stomach and grinned. "I'm a growing boy. But I'll make a sacrifice for you. I'll share." He picked up the chocolate bar, which he knew was her favorite kind, waved it in front of her, then held it out to her, inviting her to take it from his hand.

She shook her head. "I'm on a diet. Thanks anyway."

His eyes narrowed. While Shannon had never been thin, she certainly wasn't fat. If he had learned one thing over the years, it was never to make comments about a woman's weight, except to ask if they'd lost some. He'd bought the chocolate bar especially for her as a peace offering, but apparently, she wasn't going to make it easy for him, not that he deserved easy. "Take it. If you feel you need to work it off we can go jogging, or I'll challenge you to a game of tennis after work. I promise I'll let you win."

She rolled her eyes, then took a sip of her tea, some herbal blend he absolutely hated but couldn't recall the name. He knew the box was green. And a box of it just happened to be in his cupboard, in case he could ever convince her to set foot in his door.

"I don't think so."

The young clerk piped up. "I'll go jogging or play tennis with you after work, Todd."

Todd cleared his throat. He didn't really want to do either. After work, he wanted only to go home, sit back on the couch, and put his feet up, especially if he could get Shannon to relax with him. He'd even make her a cup of that horrid tea.

He turned and smiled at the girl, wishing he could remember her name. "Sorry. I was just kidding. I'm going straight home after work."

Todd thought it best to be quiet as he ate his sandwich, then the carrots, the muffin, and the apple, while the ladies around him nibbled at their salads. They sipped their coffee and tea, and Todd chugged down a pint of chocolate milk.

When lunchtime was over, the others gathered their belongings, and Todd tossed his empty containers into his lunch tote. The sound of Shannon's voice beside him almost made him miss his last shot before he snapped the lid shut.

"Honestly, Todd—I don't know where you put all that food."

He grinned and patted his stomach again. "I told you I'm a growing boy."

She rolled her eyes. "That's for sure."

Without another word, she returned to her desk.

Todd lowered his chin so no one could see him smiling. She spoke to him without his initiating it. He was making progress.

❧

It had taken two weeks, and his only improvement was that when he smiled or said hello she would smile back.

Two long weeks. Todd didn't want to calculate how long it would take to get a warm response. What he wanted most was for her to see he'd changed. He wanted to ask her out. He wanted to share his joys and his sorrows with her, and for her to do the same. He wanted to be close enough to pray with her. Not the general prayer and praise items he heard at the large Bible study he attended weekly. He wanted to know the things near her heart. And when they had nothing to say, he wanted to be able to enjoy a companionable silence, to be comfortable together without the need for words.

He wanted to touch her without her cringing, thinking he was going to tickle or jab her. He wanted to hold her the way a man holds a woman, to hold her tight and bury his face in her hair and tell her he loved her and hear she loved him, too.

He wanted to win her confidence and earn her trust, something he hadn't done before.

He needed advice.

Usually, he asked Craig for help, especially lately. This time, however, he deemed it wise not to talk to Craig about how to get close to his sister. Todd valued his life.

He went home and prayed for an answer.

three

"Good morning, Shannon."

"Good morning, Todd."

To Shannon's surprise, Todd didn't stop to linger as they crossed paths on the way to their desks. He merely smiled and continued on his way into the dispatch office, coffee mug in hand. Shannon couldn't decide if she was disappointed or not. It was the start of the third week of being in close proximity for eight hours a day, and so far, to the untrained eye, all had appeared normal. Todd had not brought up past experiences, nor had he been overly familiar with her in front of the rest of the staff. He treated her exactly the same as everyone else. And she didn't know what to make of it.

Shannon rested her mug of hot tea on the corner of her desk as she sat down, then opened the drawer to get her pencil. Instead of the pencil, she found a roll of white paper tied with a bright red ribbon. What looked like a chocolate kiss wrapped in foil was knotted to the ribbon. Shannon glanced from side to side, and when she was certain no one was looking, she untied the ribbon and read the note.

> *Dearest Shannon,*
> *Roses are red,*
> *Violets are blue.*
> *Chocolate is sweet,*
> *And so are you.*
>
> *Your Secret Admirer*

Shannon reread the note then dropped it, along with the

ribbon and the candy, back into the drawer. She slammed the drawer shut.

Dearest Shannon? Secret Admirer?

She couldn't imagine who would do such a thing. Whoever the joker was, Shannon didn't consider it very funny. Her first suspect was Todd, but this wasn't his style. There was no obvious punch line. Anonymous frogs were his style, not sweet little personal notes presented with candy. Besides she had just walked in with him. Todd received great satisfaction from watching the recipients of his little jokes, but he had stepped right past her, straight into the dispatch area, just as he had every other day in the past two weeks.

As discreetly as she could, without moving her head, Shannon once more studied the office. Still no one was watching, so she slowly opened the drawer and delicately picked off the foil wrapping.

It looked like chocolate.

She picked it up.

It felt like chocolate. It smelled like chocolate. She cautiously bit the tip off. It even tasted like chocolate. In fact she recognized the chocolate. This was not from the bulk bin at the grocery store. This was from her favorite specialty shop. At first, she thought it had to be from someone who knew her fairly well, but then decided it was just a coincidence. Lots of people loved this particular brand; that was how the store stayed in business.

All day, not a soul acted any differently toward her, nor did anyone exhibit any suspicious behavior. By the end of the day, Shannon managed to shrug it off, chalking it up to one of life's little mysteries.

❧

Tuesday morning, after relaxing with an early cup of tea in the lunchroom with a few of the other women, Shannon headed for her desk. She sat down, set her mug on the corner of the desk as she had every other morning; but when she reached to open her drawer, she hesitated.

Shannon bit back a smile. Yesterday was an isolated incident. She just hadn't figured out the person or the punch line.

Shannon opened the drawer and caught her breath. Another note lay in her pencil tray. White paper tied with a red ribbon, chocolate kiss attached. Before she touched it, not bothering to be discreet, she spun around in her chair and blatantly studied everyone in the office. Fewer people were in the office than yesterday this early, and all of them were women. Faye lifted her head, made eye contact, then returned to her work.

Shannon concentrated on the little white piece of paper. Quickly, she pulled the ribbon off, left the chocolate kiss in the tray, and unrolled the paper.

Dearest Shannon,
   A chocolate kiss
   Makes me think of you.
   I hope that now
   This will remind you of me, too.
                 Your Secret Admirer

Shannon's heart raced as she scrunched the paper in her hand and glanced around the room. The words *"Dearest Shannon"* echoed in her head as sharply as if she'd heard them out loud. She contemplated the possibility of another woman named Shannon being hidden somewhere in the building. Whoever the man was, his sentiments were romantic, even if his pentameter wasn't quite right.

"Hey, Shan-nooze. Did you see the hockey game on TV last night? The Leafs won." Todd approached from the lunchroom, holding his coffee mug.

Shannon fumbled with the note, shoved it back in the pencil tray, and slammed the drawer shut. Here was one man who knew better than to call her sweet. Over the years, one of the few activities she had managed to participate in with her brother and his friends, Todd included, was to play hockey with them. She was the best forward among them, and she never let them forget it.

"Yes, it was a good game," she mumbled.

The same as the day before, Todd didn't stop to chat. Once again, he simply disappeared through the doorway into the dispatch office. The man was going to drive her crazy.

Last night, she'd had a long talk with Craig. She didn't know how it happened, but a major portion of their conversation centered around Todd.

Craig had been accompanying Todd to the Bible study she used to attend when she lived at home. Shannon wanted to hear more, but Craig didn't tell her anything she hadn't heard before. Craig said Todd took his faith seriously and was now living a good Christian life, which meant both in and out of church.

She tried to prod Craig for information on what Todd thought of the two of them working together, but Craig didn't know. He said Todd deliberately avoided that topic.

Shannon found it difficult to focus on her work. Out of the corner of her eye, she watched everyone around her, testing their reactions as she purposely mentioned her favorite brand of chocolate kisses in every conversation. No one acted any different than any other day.

She tried to limit the possibilities of who the note writer could be; but when she counted the single male members of the office staff, the dispatch office, the foremen, warehousemen, and drivers, the list seemed endless. She didn't think most of them even knew her name; they only knew her as the payroll clerk. But all it took was one.

By the time she went home for the evening, she was still no closer to a solution.

❧

Wednesday morning, Shannon deliberately arrived at work early. She didn't linger in the lunchroom. She didn't take time to make a cup of tea.

Shannon hustled to her desk and opened the drawer.

Another white paper lay rolled up in her pencil tray, again tied with a red ribbon and accompanied by a chocolate kiss. Her hands shook as she tugged the ribbon open.

> *Dearest Shannon,*
> > *Your happy smile*
> > *Shines every day.*
> > *You are more special*
> > *Than words can say.*
> > > *Your Secret Admirer*

Shannon nearly choked. She wasn't special. She was ordinary. Very ordinary. Nor could she figure out who in the world would think she was special, except her parents, who didn't count in this instance.

She tried to determine who had access to her desk, and the answer was everyone.

Apparently, some detective work was in order. The first and most logical step would be to ask, without giving away details, if other office staff had seen anyone lingering around her desk. It would take only two seconds, though, to open her drawer, slip something in and close it. A person wouldn't have to slow down very much when walking past. Employees dropped time cards and medical forms on her desk all the time. Some even opened her drawer freely to borrow her pens if she wasn't there and they needed to leave her a note.

She decided not to ask questions of the men, in case she

asked the person who had actually left the note. Most of all she didn't want people talking. She only wanted to find out who was doing this.

Footsteps sounded behind her. Todd, with his usual morning coffee in hand, was on his way to the dispatch office.

"Todd, may I ask you something?"

He shuffled the mug from one hand to the other. "Ouch, ouch! I can't stop now. I overfilled my coffee, and it's spilling on my fingers. Maybe later."

Muttering under his breath and leaving a trail of coffee dribbles on the floor, Todd disappeared through the dispatch office doorway.

For a moment, Shannon had considered that Todd could be on her list of suspects, but she now mentally crossed him off. He could have saved his fingers from further harm by resting the coffee mug on her desk and talking to her for a minute or two before resuming his journey. But he didn't. He'd kept right on going, not even looking at her as he balanced his too-full coffee mug.

Oddly, his actions gave Shannon a strange sensation in the pit of her stomach. She wondered if he had intended to give her a taste of her own medicine by virtually ignoring her. He'd done exactly to her what she'd been doing to him since they had begun working together. Intentional or not, it gave her a stab of guilt, now knowing what it felt like to be passed by.

Shannon continued to stare at the doorway long after Todd disappeared from sight. He hadn't deserved to be treated the way she'd been treating him. Since they had been working together, he had been friendly and courteous. No one who saw them together would know of their shaky past relationship. For once, he was acting mature, which made her wonder if perhaps Craig could be right. Perhaps Todd had changed.

Shannon blinked hard a couple of times and shifted her gaze to a blank spot on the wall. What was she thinking? Just as in the past, no matter how much she hoped and prayed he would change, Todd was still Todd.

The warehouse supervisor *thunked* a pile of time cards on the corner of her desk, interrupting her mental meanderings. Shannon returned her thoughts to her job.

The whole day, she didn't venture far from her desk. Whenever she did leave, she watched it out of the corner of her eye. To her dismay, no one came within touching distance of it when she was nearby, except to drop off more time cards or mail. Short of video surveillance, she didn't know what else to do.

Not wanting to waste any more time, she gave up trying and buried herself in the stacks of papers and time cards.

❧

Shannon flipped the page on her desk calendar. Today was Thursday. She didn't want to know what was inside her drawer. But before she could begin her work she had to get her pencil. She couldn't sit and stare at the closed drawer all day.

Taking in a deep breath for courage, Shannon yanked the drawer open. Sure enough, another note awaited her. With trembling fingers, she pulled open the ribbon.

> *Dearest Shannon,*
> > *You're sweet, you're kind,*
> > *You're very smart.*
> > *Just by being you,*
> > *You've won my heart.*
> > > *Your Secret Admirer*

A sick feeling rolled through Shannon's stomach. Whoever this Secret Admirer was, she worried in earnest that he was serious. What scared her more than anything was that she had no idea who he might be.

She needed help. Except she didn't know whom to ask.

She had already figured out she couldn't ask any of the men. Nor did she want to ask the women in her immediate vicinity. She was too embarrassed to tell anyone what was happening and too afraid they would start to gossip.

The only person she could trust was good ol' Todd. Being a man, Todd might overhear talk amongst the other men. If she was lucky, Mr. Secret Admirer might let a few things slip—if someone knew what to listen for.

The key would be Todd. Once she told him what was going on, she knew he'd keep her secret. Shannon could weasel almost any information out of Craig. But she'd never stood a chance with Todd, which was probably one of the reasons he was so successful at his many escapades.

For the first time since Todd started working at Kwiki Kouriers, Shannon could hardly wait for his arrival.

This time, however, when Todd walked through the main office on his way to the dispatch area, he wasn't alone; he was deep in conversation with Gary, his supervisor. Shannon couldn't interrupt, especially with such a delicate personal matter. It would have been bad enough if any of her female coworkers found out, but she certainly didn't want any of the men to know, least of all, Gary. Gary had asked her out a few times, and she'd turned him down so she didn't want him to suspect a potential romance was growing right under his nose, even if it was one-sided.

By the time Shannon had an opportunity to talk to Todd alone, she'd lost her courage. Years ago, she knew he would have laughed at her trepidation about an unknown suitor attempting to woo her from a distance, since she wasn't the romantic type.

Still, the notes and the effort the Secret Admirer was making touched her heart in a strange way. She didn't want to hurt the man; she only wanted him to stop.

She wanted to think Todd would understand why she felt that way, but she wasn't sure he would. Not that Todd was completely insensitive; she had seen occasional flickers of a gentle side, especially since he'd been working there. She simply decided he wouldn't understand why she couldn't let it run its course and stop.

She figured he'd tell her to enjoy it, too. Todd had always had an insatiable need for attention. He didn't know when to quit, and he often created a scene when he knew people were watching him. Shannon didn't like to be the center of attention. She just wanted to be left alone, and that included anonymous romantic notes.

Shannon flipped the page on her desk calendar. It was Friday. Only one more day until the weekend when she could either put this foolishness behind her or spend some serious time trying to figure out the identity of her mysterious admirer. For a second, she considered coming in over the weekend and dusting for fingerprints.

Sure enough, Shannon found another note in her drawer, as she had the previous four days.

After she made a cursory check to see if anyone was watching, she untied the bow, popped the chocolate kiss into her mouth, and opened the roll of paper.

This time the note wasn't a poem at all; it was a message, and it was longer. Rather than take the chance that someone would see it in walking by, she quickly folded it, stuck it in her pocket, ran into the ladies' washroom, and shut the door. She dug the note out of her pocket.

Dearest Shannon,

As you can tell by now, I'm not very good at writing poetry, so I will simply tell you what is in my heart. You are sweet and wonderful, and your laugh warms my soul like the spring sunshine, filling me with hope and happiness. Please keep smiling.

Your Secret Admirer

Shannon's lower lip quivered, and she brushed a tear away from her eye. Who was this man, and why was he doing this? Did he think she might scorn him if he asked her out? A couple of the men besides Gary had asked her for a date, and it was true she had turned them down, but she had done it kindly. She didn't want to be yoked with an unbeliever, so she didn't open the potential for heartbreak by dating someone who didn't share her faith.

She read the note again, then refolded it and tucked it in her pocket.

She would have to dig seriously for clues.

The first would be handwriting comparisons. Monday morning she would come in early. Not only did she have access to people's payroll forms and files, but she also had access to all the time cards. She could start by comparing signatures and see if that would give her some indication of who this could be.

She would solve this mystery, and when she found out who was behind it she would—

Shannon shook her head. The first few notes were kind of silly, but the last note had touched her heart. It exuded a simple honesty that told her the sender was, indeed, serious. It was flattering beyond belief that someone thought so much of her yet was so shy he would resort to this.

For the rest of the day, Shannon buried herself in her work. Over the weekend, she would devise a plan to discover the sender of the notes, as well as figure out what she would say to this person. But for now, she had a payroll deadline to meet.

❧

Todd walked to his car ahead of Shannon, waved at her as

they started their engines, and waved again to signal her to go ahead of him. When she was out of the parking lot, Todd shut off his engine and returned to the building.

The only remaining employees at this hour were in the dispatch office and warehouse, and everyone was running around at what was always the busiest time of the day. The drivers were lined up at the bay doors, bringing everything in for distribution to be organized for delivery the next business day. As usual, Friday night was the busiest of all.

He could have danced in with colored spotlights, wearing a clown suit, and whistling Dixie. No one would have given him a second glance. And that was just the way he wanted it.

Todd walked to Shannon's desk, opened her drawer, dropped in another note, chocolate kiss attached, and left the building.

four

"Excuse me. I was supposed to be in early today."

Faye stepped back for Todd, allowing him to stand beside Shannon while he filled his mug with coffee and Shannon poured boiled water from the kettle into her mug.

Todd winked at Faye over his shoulder, then turned to smile at Shannon while he deliberately overfilled his coffee mug. Balancing it carefully, he slowly began his trek through the office on the way to his station. Mentally, he counted out the time Shannon would take to dunk her tea bag in the water until it was the right color and toss the tea bag into the garbage pail.

Picturing her task completed, he sloshed coffee over the edge of his mug to make a large splash on the floor. He grumbled loud enough for everyone in the vicinity to hear, set his cup down on the nearest desk, and returned to the lunchroom. His timing was perfect. He met Shannon in the doorway as she was on her way out, and he was on the way in.

He stepped to the side to allow her to pass. "I spilled some coffee on the floor. Don't trip. I need a paper towel."

"Serves you right for cutting in front of Faye."

He winked at her, enjoying the slight blush. "She didn't mind." He dropped his voice to a whisper. "I think she likes me."

Shannon mumbled something under her breath he didn't think he wanted to hear and headed across the room to her desk.

Todd hurried back into the lunchroom. While he tugged a few paper towels from the holder, he calculated the seconds Shannon would take to set her mug on the corner of her desk and walk around it as she always did. Once back in the office area, he smiled at the ladies who were nearby as he returned to the splotch on the floor. He squatted down to wipe it at the same time Shannon sat in her chair. He had deliberately spilled his coffee where he would have an unencumbered view of her as she opened her drawer.

From his vantage point near the floor he watched as she hesitated. She turned her head ever so slightly from side to side to see if anyone was watching, which fortunately didn't include him, even though she was aware he was there. She pulled the drawer open.

He heard her soft intake of breath when she saw the note. Again, her head moved from side to side. She paused and gently pulled the ribbon open. Todd's heart pounded as he mentally recited the words he'd worked so hard to write.

> *Dearest Shannon,*
> *Monday is here, the weekend is gone.*
> *Which is good, because Saturday and Sunday were much too long.*
> *My heart ached with loss. I didn't know what to do.*
> *I couldn't see your smile from home, and I missed you.*
> *Your Secret Admirer*

Moving ever so slowly, she tucked the note back into the drawer.

Todd lowered his head and smiled to himself as he swiped the paper towel over the floor one last time. She didn't throw the note in the garbage can, and she was eating the chocolate kiss, meaning that so far all was well.

He stood, tossed the paper towel into the nearest wastepaper basket, and picked up his mug. He slurped some coffee off the top, then began walking toward the dispatch office.

Shannon raised her head and looked straight at him. "Todd, may I ask you something?"

His heart stopped, then started up in double time. The only reason she would want to talk to him would be to ask him about the note she had just read. He wasn't ready to talk about the note or any of the others before it. He hadn't even completely figured out what he was going to say, day after day. He simply wanted to keep telling Shannon how special she was and that she held his heart in the palm of her hand. Not that she would fall in love with him just because he wrote bad poetry. His goal was to prove he was serious and really did love her, despite the rotten and immature things he'd done to her in the past. Hopefully, when the time came for him to reveal himself, they could put the past behind them and move forward into a real relationship.

But he couldn't talk about any of that now. He was already nervous about what he was doing and still not confident it would work. In fact, he was afraid he might blurt out how he felt if she confronted him. He didn't want that to happen in the middle of the office. Most of all, he didn't know if he could handle her rejection.

He wrapped his fingers around his mug, glanced at the door to the dispatch area, then turned back to Shannon. "Gary wanted me here early today to go over some special requests for a new customer. How about if I catch you at lunchtime?"

Her posture sagged, not much, but just enough to note her disappointment. "I guess. I'll see you later then."

Todd walked to his station as quickly as he could with his full coffee mug. He almost had to push the image of Shannon reading his latest note out of his mind so he could begin his perusal of the paperwork Gary had already spread out over the counter.

He was now starting the fourth week of his job. He was familiar with procedures, better acquainted with the rest of the staff, and confident enough in his abilities that he was comfortable working there.

The words on the papers blurred before him. After seeing Shannon every day, he was also more in love with her than ever before.

But, before he could think any more about Shannon, Gary appeared beside him. He rested his finger on one of the requests their new customer had stipulated before signing the contract. During their last meeting, they had been trying to determine if the expense of paying the overtime needed to fulfill the request would be worth it to secure the new business. "We've got everything covered except for this. What do you think?"

Todd cleared his throat, which helped clear his thoughts. "If we can convince Charlie to take his coffee break half an hour later, then we can send him here"—he pointed on the map to an area on one of the other drivers' runs—"and send Tyler in the other direction. With the slight delay, we can send Charlie to the industrial park, then to their new warehouse in the new development. That way, we can meet their schedule without compromising the other appointments. We can get Bob and Hank to do the rest of Charlie's run and use hired cartage or a part-timer to do what Bob and Hank leave behind. That would eliminate the need for any overtime."

Gary rubbed his chin. "I never thought of that. That would work. Great idea."

Todd suppressed his smile. "Thanks," he mumbled, trying not to look like a child receiving praise from his favorite teacher.

Gary gathered the papers and began sorting them back into order. "I see you're friendly with Shannon," he said, without looking at Todd. He paused, letting the silence hang.

Todd's satisfaction for a job well done dropped as heavily as a lead balloon. He didn't know why the relationship he had with Shannon was any of his supervisor's concern, but Gary's continued silence told him he was waiting for clarification.

Todd turned to study the man. He didn't know what Shannon thought of him. He only knew Gary and Shannon appeared to share nothing more than a companionable working relationship. But Todd wasn't stupid or blind. Even though Gary, as the operations manager, spent much of his time in his office, he also worked with Todd and the other two dispatchers. While the men worked, they talked.

Bryan was happily married with a baby on the way, but Gary and Rick were both single. Being single, and not Christians, they talked a lot about women, not all of which Todd wanted to hear. So far, he'd heard a few of their opinions of the women who worked in the office, some complimentary, some not. Fortunately, not much had been said about Shannon, probably because it was obvious he knew her prior to working there. He had a bad feeling that was about to change.

"Yeah, I've known her for years. Why?"

"Just wondering. I saw you talking to her again this morning. I was wondering if you two had anything going—that's all."

The short conversation he'd had with Shannon raced through his head. They'd said nothing of significance, only that they would talk again at lunchtime.

Todd continued to watch Gary, who was still fiddling with the papers in the folder. After listening to Rick and Gary for the past three weeks, Todd knew Rick made it a policy never to date women at work, just in case things ended badly and they had to see each other every day. But Gary had no such standards or considerations. He had dated Jody, a woman in the credit department, for awhile. Every time Jody and Gary were in the lunchroom at the same time, Jody began acting strange. Gary, on the other hand, showed no signs of awkwardness, aversion, or regret. He didn't know Gary well enough yet to know if that was good or bad.

As much as he wanted to know why Gary was asking, unless Todd could claim something more positive than Shannon's finally being able to stay in the same room with him without wanting to run after three minutes, he had no grounds to suggest a relationship that wasn't there.

He tried to make it sound as good as he could without lying. "We're old friends from back when we were kids." At least Shannon had been a kid and just part of the package of his friendship with Craig. But now, he kicked himself for not appreciating what could have developed between them, if he had treated her with the respect she deserved.

He fought back a grin at the last time he'd teased her about playing hockey with the big boys. She'd defiantly given him a hip check as potent as any of the guys. He'd had a bruise for a week to remind him she didn't just deserve the respect; she demanded it.

Todd became serious as he turned his thoughts back to his supervisor. Gary's sudden questions were starting to worry him.

"So you know her pretty well then?"

Todd tried to keep his expression casual. He knew Shannon well enough that he would marry her tomorrow, if she'd have him, which at this point she wouldn't. But if his words on paper could open her heart to accept the new man he had become, then, sometime in the future, living with her forever as man and wife might be a real possibility. He knew what she liked and didn't like, and he loved her more than life itself.

He cleared his throat. "I know her very well, actually."

"Anything else?"

Todd opened his mouth, but no words came out. He wanted to tell Gary that he and Shannon were going to be bound together until the end of time, except that Shannon had only recently began speaking to him again. He was stuck—for the time being.

"By the way," Gary added before Todd could answer, "if you're not, you know, doing anything with Shan, I think Faye's pretty interested in you."

Inwardly, Todd cringed. He knew Faye had a crush on

him. He also knew she wasn't a Christian. Shannon's faith through the years, in good times and bad, was one of the many things he loved about her. Even if she never returned his feelings, he wouldn't go out with someone who didn't share his faith. He tried to be kind to Faye without encouraging her. While he was flattered by her attentions, he wasn't interested. He was interested only in Shannon.

He didn't quite know how to handle Gary yet, but he did know that humor had always worked for him. Todd splayed both hands over his heart and sighed melodramatically. "I know about Faye, but my heart belongs to another."

Gary rolled his eyes. "You've been watching too many cheap chick flicks. I think you have some work to do."

Todd gladly picked up his book of notes to follow up on, sat at his station, and lifted the phone to dial. He had never been so glad to get to work.

By the time the lunch hour arrived, Todd was more than ready. Like every other day, he was alone in the dispatch office for half an hour while Rick and Bryan went for lunch. Gary was in his office catching up on the morning's happenings, but he was prepared to come into the dispatch area if the phones went wild while Todd was alone.

Fortunately for Todd, everything remained quiet, and for now, his paperwork was done. He'd finished the routing for the pickup requests received so far. Even most of the drivers were now officially off for their break.

Line 3 was lit up. He glanced over his shoulder to see that Gary was on the phone. As long as the light was on, Gary would remain in his office.

As usual at this time, Todd had nothing to do but watch the wall. He began to write the note Shannon would read on Tuesday morning.

Dearest Shannon,

The pen froze. He knew she had become more curious about the sender of the notes because she was going to talk to him about it, until he put her off.

Todd looked down at his own handwriting. He didn't want the notes to be perceived as threatening in any way so he had decided to handwrite them, to give them a friendly and personal touch, instead of typing them on his computer and printing them. But now, staying anonymous had become more of an issue. As far as he knew, Shannon had never seen his handwriting. Since he was salaried and not hourly, he didn't fill out a time sheet at the end of the week. When the drivers had overtime, he initialed their time cards, but that was only a scribbled *TS*, which he usually did standing, without a solid surface behind them. His initials were not even close to use as a comparable handwriting sample.

The only official documents on file with his handwriting written legibly were the job application he had filled out and the IRS form. Shannon was the payroll administrator, but he didn't think she had access to those files. Even if she did, she had too much honor to search through personnel files for handwriting samples.

He looked at the customers' routing cards sorted neatly in the various drivers' route slots. The names of their customers were written in, but he wasn't the only one doing it. Gary and the other dispatchers wrote in the names, and sometimes people in the office wrote an occasional pickup request. As well, the times the calls were given to the drivers were noted by whoever was on the radio to that driver at the time, which was any one of the four of them. At the end of the day, all the cards were gathered into a bundle, labeled by date, and tossed into a box, never to be looked at again unless there was a problem. It wasn't likely Shannon would ever look there. Even if she did dig through the box and match the handwriting, nothing was identifiable as his.

Todd smiled and continued writing.

Every day while we're at work,

Todd stopped writing. His brain stalled while he tried to think of a word that rhymed with "work." Since nothing came, he mentally ran through the alphabet starting with A, taking each letter and ending it with the "erk" sound. The first combination he made that was really a word was "jerk," so he kept going. The next word started with the letter L, but he didn't think it was a good idea to mention the word "lurk" in a note. He was already leaving anonymous notes, and he didn't want to frighten Shannon or hint that he was following her around. He wasn't a stalker. He only wanted to tell her he recognized the special Christian woman she'd become and how much he loved her.

He crumpled the paper and shoved it in his pocket to put through the shredder, then started again.

Dearest Shannon,
Thinking of you makes me smile,
Like. . .

The pen froze again. What happy thing rhymed with smile? He started to run through the alphabet again, mentally choked on the word "bile," shook his head and kept going with the alphabet.

Like an alligator in the lazy Nile.

Or was it crocodiles in the Nile? He knew alligators lived in Florida and crocodiles lived in Australia, but he didn't know which ones lived in Egypt.

Todd scribbled out the words and shoved that piece of paper in his pocket, too. He didn't want her to think he was a predatory animal. He'd already nixed another predatory word.

Todd started again.

Dearest Shannon,

The phone rang before he could think of another opening sentence. He chatted with the caller for a few minutes while noting some special requests for a pickup of a priority parcel, then resumed his quest.

The light went out for line 3. The scrape of Gary's chair along the tile floor was followed by the metallic grind of his filing-cabinet drawer opening. "Almost ready?" Gary called out. "Those guys should be back soon."

Todd looked up at the clock. He had five minutes left in which to write the note he would leave tomorrow.

He gritted his teeth. Writing poetry was hard enough, but writing good, meaningful, sincere poetry was even harder, especially when he had to do it while watching the clock.

Dearest Shannon,
   I love you more every day
   You are more special than words can say

He stopped writing, fighting for the words as every tick of the clock echoed loudly through his head, reminding him time was running short.

Nothing came. Bryan's and Rick's voices drifted through the doorway, signaling their imminent arrival.

Todd folded the paper carefully and shoved it in his pocket. His only option to finish the note in private would be to do it in the washroom before he left. He told himself this was what he deserved for not writing the note at home, when he had more time and the privacy he needed. His struggles also served as a reminder that the more notes he wrote, the harder it was becoming to find different wording and more rhymes he hadn't used before.

It was a lot of work, and he knew he had to be diligent, but this was the only way he could think of to tell Shannon how he felt. When the time was right to reveal himself, he hoped she would see that for once in his life his actions toward her were sincere and she would take him seriously.

·❧·

Shannon set her mug on the corner of her desk, walked around to her chair, and slid in.

When she reached for the drawer handle, she realized she would be disappointed if she didn't find a new note.

She held her breath, wrapped her fingers around the cold metal, and pulled. Sure enough, another note lay in the pencil tray.

As she picked up the small piece of notepaper, again bound by a red ribbon with a chocolate kiss tied to the end, she paused. This note wasn't as pristine as the other notes. For the first time, the paper was crinkled.

She shrugged her shoulders, tugged the bow on the ribbon to open it, set the chocolate kiss aside, and began to read.

> *Dearest Shannon,*
> > *I love you more every day*
> > *You are more special than words can say.*
> > *These words I write are to say to you*
> > *That I think of you in all I do.*
> > > *Your Secret Admirer*

Shannon smiled. The Secret Admirer's poetry was still bad, but his sentiments continued to be just as sweet.

She put the paper down in front of her and picked up the chocolate kiss. As she picked off the colored foil wrapping, she reread the note, trying to figure out if the word patterns were familiar or if any expressions might be unique to one person. She had almost finished the last line when she heard footsteps behind her chair. She quickly whipped the note into her drawer, grabbed her pencil, and popped the chocolate kiss into her mouth.

"I saw that," Faye said as she appeared beside Shannon.

Shannon's heart pounded. She had thought she'd tucked the note away soon enough, but she'd become careless. She turned to the side and looked up at Faye, who was standing beside her chair and holding a mug of steaming coffee in one hand. Shannon's voice dropped to a whisper. "Please don't tell anyone."

Faye's eyebrows raised. "Why? Are you on a diet? You of all people, too." She rested her free hand on her stomach. "I'm the one who could probably lose ten pounds, but not you."

Shannon tried not to sag with relief that it was only the chocolate Faye had seen. She said the first thing that came to her mind. "I guess it's just a girl thing. Next weekend I'm going to an anniversary celebration at my old church, and I want to be able to fit into my dress."

Faye picked up the foil wrapping. "It was just a chocolate kiss, not a whole bar. How many calories can it have?" She glanced around Shannon's desktop, then to the drawer, which was tightly closed. "Got any more? Do you share?"

"Sorry. I only got one."

Faye turned and looked at her own desk, beside Shannon's, which was bare except for her in and out baskets and computer. "Got? You mean someone around here has good chocolate kisses and skipped me? I'm going to have to wring someone's neck. Who's giving them out?"

Shannon nearly choked, even though the last of the kiss had already dissolved in her mouth. Her mind raced to think of what she could say that wouldn't be lying but yet wouldn't be spilling the beans about what had been happening for over a week now. "I don't know. Someone left it for me." She deliberately didn't mention the notes that came with the kisses and hoped and prayed Faye wouldn't ask for more details.

"Wow. Someone has a crush on you, I'll bet."

Shannon had a bad feeling it was more than a crush, since someone was going to a lot of trouble and for so long. "Naw. It's probably just someone who knows I like this kind of chocolate. I'll bet they're even wondering why I haven't thanked them. I should probably know who it is, but I can't figure it out."

Faye sighed, her eyes drifted shut, and she pressed her free hand over her heart. "I wish some handsome knight would woo me with chocolate kisses. He'd have my heart for sure." Her eyes opened, and she grinned at Shannon. "I'd really like it if Todd would leave me romantic stuff like that."

"Todd?" Shannon blinked. The only thing he'd ever left her was a cold, slimy live frog. "That man doesn't have a romantic bone in his body. Don't tell me you have a crush on him." His remark from the previous day—that he thought Faye liked him—repeated in her head. It appeared he was right.

"He's so–o–o handsome. And so funny!"

"He's also. . ." Shannon's voice trailed off. Todd was funny, when a person wasn't the target of his jokes. And she couldn't argue that he wasn't handsome, because he was. The biggest problem was he knew it.

She tried to think of something else to say about Todd to discourage Faye, to tell her what he was really like, but again, she had to be fair. They'd worked together for nearly a month, and he'd done nothing untoward. He hadn't played a single practical joke on anyone. He was polite, helpful, and appeared to be doing a good job. If she had to draw a dotted line in time, from the day he started working there, she couldn't think of anything bad to say about him.

As well, Todd continued to be her brother's best friend after fifteen years. Craig always chose his friends carefully. He had many acquaintances but only a select group of people he would call close friends. Craig said repeatedly that Todd had turned his life around and changed into a decent human being.

Faye waited expectantly beside her. "Todd's also. . . ?"

"Nothing," Shannon mumbled as she typed in her password and opened her e-mail. "I forgot what I was going to say. Just remember that even though Todd isn't bad looking, beauty is only skin deep."

Faye nodded. She began to walk the three steps to her desk but stopped after only two steps. She turned her head to look over her shoulder at Shannon. "That may be so, but beauty is also in the eye of the beholder."

five

Todd walked into the bookstore, trying to make it look as if he were comfortable in such a place. He stared up and down one aisle, then another, unable to believe there could be so many books under one roof. They even had a coffee shop in the back. The public library hadn't been as large as this store.

The book he'd wanted had been marked "library use only," and he couldn't go into the library every few days. Therefore, he had come to buy the book.

If he could find it.

A young lady wearing a green polo shirt with a pin-on badge showing the logo of the store and the name "Staci" approached him, proving he looked as lost as he felt.

"May I help you?" she asked.

He didn't know if he should admit he'd just been to the library, where he didn't have to pay for anything. "I'm looking for one of those books that has rhyming words in it. For writing stuff."

She smiled politely. "You mean a rhyming dictionary? We have a number of different kinds. There are rhyming dictionaries for both children and adults. Some are geared for poets. We have a nice one for musicians—and a few in more of a dictionary format. We have them in paperback or hardcover."

Todd's head swam. If it wasn't hard enough to pick meaningful words that rhymed and still get his point across, now he had to decide which reference book was the best kind to suit his needs. The one he'd found at the library seemed good, but he hadn't realized it was any specific kind. He only knew he couldn't leave the building with it. "Yeah," he mumbled. "That's what I want."

She pointed across the room. "In the nonfiction section, in 18B."

"Thanks," he mumbled again and began walking.

When he finally found the right shelf, he gritted his teeth and went through all of the books, one by one, until he found one that looked as if it had the biggest selection of words per page. He cringed at the price, now realizing why the library wouldn't let their copy out of the building, then picked a smaller paperback version instead. For what he was doing, he didn't need every word in the English language. He only needed lists of words that rhymed.

With his selection in hand, Todd headed toward the front of the store to check out. While he walked, he continued to survey the building and its contents, feeling more in awe with every table and shelf he passed. Finally, when he came to a table displaying a big yellow sign that announced everything on it was marked seventy percent off, his curiosity got the better of him. He stopped.

The subject of most of the books centered on past holiday seasons. Some were works of fiction by authors he had never heard of before. When he saw one title that contained the word "Bible" he picked it up. He turned it over and started reading the back cover to discover the book was a work of fiction based on the life of one of the Old Testament prophets.

Todd couldn't remember the last time he read anything that wasn't nonfiction or was longer than a magazine article. He opened the book and started to read the first page to see if he might like it when a voice piped up beside him.

"Todd? What are you doing here?"

He fumbled with the book, snapped it shut, and slipped it over the rhyming dictionary to hide the title.

"Shannon," he muttered, trying to keep his voice from cracking. "What are you doing here?"

She glanced at the table, then at the two books in his hand.

"The same thing as you, apparently."

Shannon, too, held a couple of books. From as far back as he knew her, he remembered her reading something. He shouldn't have been surprised to find her in a bookstore.

She lowered her head to look at his two books and tipped her head slightly. "What do you have? Anything interesting?"

He pressed the two books tightly together, not offering her either one. "I guess. Maybe. I'm not sure. What do you have?" Not that he wanted to know specifically what she was reading. He only wanted to distract her from the books in his own hand. Especially the one on the bottom.

Shannon had no such hesitations. She held out both books to him so he could plainly see the covers. "I have a couple of inspirational romance anthologies. I just love Christian fiction, and we have more to choose from now. It's especially great to find them in a store like this. You know how much I love to read. I have to admit I'm a little surprised to see you here. I can't say I've ever seen you with a book in your hand."

He grinned. For years, he'd teased her about being a bookworm. He'd only meant it as a compliment. He considered her diligence in reading to be a sign of intelligence. She always countered his teasing by calling him illiterate.

Todd cleared his throat and straightened his smile. He pressed his hand to his chest, over his heart and did his best to appear serious. "There're a lot of things about me you don't know. How about if I treat you to a coffee, and I'll tell you about them?"

She glanced at the coffee shop in the back of the store. "I don't know."

"Come on. It'll be fun."

She shrugged her shoulders. "Sure. Why not? I don't have anything better to do or anywhere else to go."

He tried not to let her comment sting, but after the things he'd said to her in the past, he probably had it coming. The important thing was that she had accepted his invitation. For that he had to be happy or at least relieved she wasn't holding a grudge. "How about if you get us a nice table, and I'll be right back. I want to pay for these first."

"Pay? But—" Once again, she glanced over her shoulder to the coffee shop then back to him. "You don't need to pay first. You're allowed to take unpaid-for books to the tables. That's how lots of people decide whether or not they're going to buy the book."

"I've already decided, so I want to pay for them first. Then I won't have to worry about forgetting." Even if he kept the sale book on top of the rhyming dictionary, she might read the title from the spine. After he paid, the dictionary would be tucked inside the bag.

She shrugged her shoulders again. "That doesn't make sense, but if that's what you want, I guess I can pay for mine, too."

He shook his head frantically. "No, I don't want to rush you. How about if you go look at the desserts and pick something good for both of us. I'll be right back." Before she could protest, he turned and walked quickly to the checkout, leaving Shannon standing beside the sale table.

Fortunately, there weren't any lines. He soon joined Shannon at the coffee shop, where she was standing in front of the display with the desserts, eyeing a selection labeled "Triple Chocolate Dream." That didn't surprise him. He almost commented on her choice but bit his tongue. He had promised himself he'd treat her with the respect she deserved and never tease her again. Besides, he didn't want to do anything to associate his knowledge for her love of chocolate to the chocolate kisses he left her every day. One day he would tell her, but only when the time was right, which wasn't now.

Todd selected something else for himself and remained silent when the clerk put their order on a tray. He paid for everything, and they moved to a table.

Shannon sipped her coffee, then nibbled the chocolate piece off the top of her dessert. Todd knew the chocolate wasn't as good a quality as the specialty kisses he'd been buying and wondered if she was comparing them. He held back his smile and drank his coffee slowly so she wouldn't notice.

After she finished the piece, she spoke. "I can't believe we've been working together for nearly a month. The time sure has gone fast, hasn't it?"

Todd nodded. "It sure has. Do you know this is the first time we've had just to sit and talk? It's almost funny we're not at work."

"I know. But you've seen by now how busy it gets in that lunchroom."

"Yeah. It's sometimes crowded in there." He smiled wryly. Even though he didn't sit with her during lunch, they often sat at the same table at coffee time, as part of a group. It wasn't what he wanted, but it was an improvement over his first week, when she wouldn't go into the lunchroom at all when he was in there.

He had to take comfort in how far they'd come since then. She was now willingly sitting with him, alone, in a friendly, semiprivate atmosphere, although he wished it could have been from something more intimate than bumping into each other at the bookstore.

"I'm actually glad to see you. I've been meaning to talk to you about something. Do you mind?"

Inwardly, he cringed. He had a bad feeling he knew what she was going to ask; only this time he couldn't run away, since sitting together for coffee was his idea. He forced himself to smile. "No, go ahead."

She leaned closer across the table. Her eyes widened, and Todd immediately became lost in their depths. The mixture of olive green and brown in her hazel eyes always fascinated him, although up until now he would never have admitted it.

"Please don't take this the wrong way, but do you know if anyone at work has a crush on me?"

His brain stalled. A little voice called for evasive maneuvers. "You mean, have I heard any of the guys talking?"

She smiled. His heart went into overdrive. "Yes. I know you're fairly new, but, well, you certainly must hear the men talk."

"I haven't heard anyone say anything about you that isn't work related, but I can try to listen if you want."

She reached toward him and rested her hand on his forearm. Her touch was gentle, even affectionate, although he knew his interpretation was probably only wishful thinking. Still, the warm contact made him hope he wouldn't break out into a cold sweat.

"That would be great. I know you think it's a strange question, but I have to know."

He blinked to clear his mind. He didn't think it was strange at all. What he did think strange was that no one else had managed to win her heart already. "Has somebody been making you nervous?"

Shannon shook her head and withdrew her hand. He almost begged her to put it back. "No. Nothing like that." She grinned and took a sip of her coffee, then spoke over the top of the cup. "Actually, someone is being very sweet. I just wish I knew who it was."

He opened his mouth, about to blurt out he was the one, but she started talking before he could formulate the words.

"In a way, it reminds me of when I was a kid and Tommy Banks had a crush on me. We were seven years old, and he bought me a chocolate bar out of his allowance; but he ate it on the way to school. Instead he made me a bookmark. I haven't received a special gift from a guy since, except for my birthday and Christmas, of course. But I still have the bookmark. He drew little red and purple hearts all over it. Do you remember Tommy?"

"Can't say that I do." What stuck in his mind, though, was not the bookmark, but her wistful comment that over the years no one else had given her anything she considered special. He'd met a few of the boys and young men she'd gone out with. He'd openly insulted every one of them, although not to their faces. She'd been angry with him every time, but he did notice that soon after he told her what he thought of her various dates and boyfriends, she broke up with them, probably because he was right. She deserved better.

But the important thing was that not one of them had given her anything she considered special that wasn't also attached to an obligatory occasion. Since she thought receiving the notes and chocolate kisses was sweet, that was reason enough for him to put his own desires aside and keep giving them to her instead of revealing himself so soon.

Before they crossed the line into dangerous territory, where being evasive might transcend into actual lying, Todd changed the subject to the upcoming twenty-fifth anniversary celebration of his church. Craig had told him Shannon would be attending both the open house on Saturday and the service on Sunday, since she'd grown up in that church. He always went to church Sunday morning, but he hadn't made up his mind about the open house Saturday night until he heard she was going. His clothes were already picked out, and he'd even ironed the pants.

He hadn't realized how much time had passed until an announcement echoed over the speakers asking shoppers to take their purchases to the checkout because the store was closing in five minutes.

Todd stood in line with Shannon so she could pay for her books. He didn't feel the least bit contrite when she teased him that he should have waited with his own purchase, since he was now standing in line a second time. In a way he found it oddly satisfying that for once she was teasing him instead of the other way around.

In fact, he couldn't remember the last time he'd enjoyed himself so much or felt so relaxed—once they stopped talking about work.

Outside, he wished he could ask her to do something so they could spend more time together, but he couldn't think of anything open at that hour on a weeknight except for the fast-food restaurants. They'd just spent the last two hours together over coffee and dessert, so she would think he was up to something if he suggested more food. Instead, he could only accompany her to her car, which was across the almost empty parking lot from his car.

He watched as she inserted the key into the lock. The time they'd spent together was the closest thing to a date he'd ever had with Shannon. Every other time they'd been together outside work, they'd traded constant banter, even insults, and were always part of a threesome, with her brother, Craig, present.

She swung the door open, tossed her purse and the bag containing the books onto the passenger seat, and started to step into the car. "I guess I'll see you at work tomorrow. 'Bye, Todd."

Todd stepped closer as she bent more to get into the car. He didn't know what they could do, but he didn't want to part ways. "Shan! Wait!"

At his words, Shannon retracted her foot, which had not yet touched the floor of the car, and backed up. "What?" she asked as she straightened. She obviously hadn't known he had moved so close to the car, because when she turned around her eyes widened when she discovered they were now only inches apart.

With the car behind her, Shannon couldn't back up. Todd didn't move. They were so close he could have simply lowered his head—and kissed her. He suddenly wanted to kiss her more than anything he'd ever wanted in his life.

"Well? Did you want something?"

"I. . .uh. . ." Todd's brain backfired. He couldn't do it. Not only would she not have expected such a thing from him, but they were in the middle of an almost deserted parking lot. He stood there with his mouth hanging open.

Shannon giggled. "What's the matter? Does calling me Shan instead of Shan-nooze when we're out of work short-circuit your vocal chords?" She raised her hands, rested her palms on his chest, and gave him a gentle nudge backward. "While I appreciate your not calling me that anymore, you're standing so close I can't focus properly. Was there something you wanted to tell me?"

He wanted to tell her he loved her. He shook his head. "It's not important. I'll see you in the morning."

Todd waited while Shannon got into her car and drove away, not moving until she'd left the lot.

He could hardly wait for morning and the start of a new day at work.

❧

Todd walked slowly into the office and looked around. Since he was earlier than usual, none of the office staff had arrived, which was what he needed. He hurried to Shannon's desk, picked up the note he'd left from the day before that was meant for her to read this morning and replaced it with a new one. He rammed the old one into his pocket, hurried into the lunchroom and began making a pot of coffee to be ready when everyone else arrived.

Just as the last drop dripped into the pot, Todd heard foot-steps in the doorway. He peeked over his shoulder, hoping it was Shannon, but it was only Gary.

"Good morning, Todd. You're in early."

"Yeah. I left a little earlier than usual, and traffic was light."

"You have good timing. You know I've given Bryan the day off. Rick called me on my cell—he's sick and won't be in. I have to go out for a meeting with a couple of new accounts in an hour. I want you to pull one of the drivers in to help with the phones and reshuffle his route. I'll see if I can get someone off the casual list to come in on short notice. Do you know where it is?"

Todd glanced up at the clock. If he was to endure a testing period to see if he was worth his salary, today would be the day. He only hoped he'd learned enough in a month to meet Gary's expectations. "I don't know. Last I saw the list, Bryan had it. I don't understand his filing system, but I can try to find it."

"Never mind. Shannon has a copy. I'll use that one," Gary said as he left the lunchroom.

Todd poured his coffee, then froze, nearly overflowing it until he realized what he was doing.

Gary was going to get the list from Shannon. But Shannon wasn't in yet.

That meant Gary was going to get into Shannon's desk.

He couldn't stop his supervisor from looking for something he legitimately needed, but Todd had his own good reasons for not wanting Gary to open her top drawer. Maybe he would only go through the bottom drawer where Shannon kept her files and nowhere else.

But Todd couldn't take the chance.

He left his mug on the counter and dashed across the lunchroom to the office. "Hey, Gary," he said, trying his best to quell the panic and sound casual as he entered the main office area. "I think I know where it is. I'll be right back."

Just as Gary straightened, Todd heard the thud of a drawer closing. Because he was looking at the front of the desk, he couldn't tell which drawer Gary had been in.

"It's okay," Gary said, holding a paper in his hand. "Shannon is very organized. I found it. Let's get busy. I have to be out of here soon."

Todd swallowed hard and returned to the lunchroom for his

coffee. He had to tell himself that since Gary's expression had been neutral, he hadn't seen the new note Todd had left for Shannon this morning. If Gary had opened the top drawer, the stark white paper with the red ribbon and red foil wrapping of the chocolate kiss would have been impossible to miss.

The phone started ringing at the same time he set his mug on the counter. He handled the call quickly, then chose a driver to help him. While Gary made a few phone calls from his office, Todd called the foreman and talked to him about pulling the priority deliveries out of Bill's truck and loading them into another. By the time Gary found a driver to replace Bill, Todd had everything under control. Or at least everything would be under control until the phones started ringing.

Gary stood beside Todd at the counter, checked the changes he'd made to the routing, and nodded. "Looks good. I have to go. Call my cell if you need me, but everything looks fine."

Todd forced himself to smile. "Yeah. See you sometime after lunch."

six

Shannon gritted her teeth as she watched a couple of the ladies from the accounts department yakking incessantly while standing in front of the lunchroom counter. She didn't want to be rude, but the kettle had boiled, and she could now make her tea. Or at least she could if she barged between them and elbowed them out of the way, which was almost what Todd had done to poor Faye the other day. Normally, she wouldn't even consider being so rude, but Shannon wanted to get to her desk.

Not that she wanted to get to work so fast. She wanted to open her drawer to see the new note of the day.

Finally, she couldn't stand it any longer. She walked forward and stepped between them to reach for the kettle, smiling politely while they stared at her in silence for interrupting them.

She dunked and redunked her tea bag, wondering if it took this long every day or if she'd somehow picked a low-quality tea bag this morning.

Even though the tea wasn't as dark as she normally liked it, Shannon tossed the bag into the trash and walked to her desk as quickly as she could without spilling anything or making it look as if she was rushing. Todd had spilled his coffee the same day he'd barged in front of Faye, and she didn't want to do the same. She had been impressed that he'd immediately wiped up his mess. Whenever the other dispatchers slopped coffee onto the floor, they let it dry, and the janitors got it when they washed the floor at night. Mostly, she didn't want anyone to notice her.

Shannon's stomach fluttered as she opened the drawer. The same as every other day for over two weeks, a little white note, fastened with a red ribbon tied to a chocolate kiss, lay in the center of her pencil tray. Keeping the note low so no one could see what she was doing, Shannon pulled the ribbon off and set the kiss aside.

Dearest Shannon,
   When I think of you I don't know where to begin
   Your magical voice is like a sweet violin.
   My heart beats with joy at the sound of your laughter,
   And your happy smile fills me with joy ever after.
                                             Your Secret Admirer

Shannon smiled. The note was tender and sweet and oddly flattering, even though the poetry itself hadn't improved. Today, though, something was different, but she couldn't quite figure out what it was.

She tucked the note into the envelope containing the other notes, unwrapped the kiss, and popped it into her mouth. While she savored the rich chocolate, Shannon turned her head toward the opening for the lunchroom. Any second now, Todd would be walking through the doorway.

She hadn't told him about the notes, but he'd promised to keep his ears open to any conversation concerning her. Of course, it was too early to hear anything. Once he arrived, she would simply remind him.

Instead of Todd, Faye walked into the office. Shannon found herself strangely disappointed.

She couldn't stop thinking about Todd. Not only had she spent the evening with him, she'd actually enjoyed herself. In many ways, he was the same old Todd she'd known since she was a kid. Yet it was the first time she'd talked to him as a single man and not as her brother's annoying friend.

Then, when they were leaving, he'd acted so strange. Todd always radiated confidence and control; yet he was at a loss for words. He'd even stammered. She didn't know what was going through his mind, but with Todd Sanders, it could have been anything. He couldn't have realized how charming his momentary lapse had been, but it showed her a side of him she didn't know existed. At the time, she'd almost been inclined to give him a hug, but since it was Todd, she'd erased the thought from her mind.

"Hi, Shan."

"Good morning, Faye. Is Todd in the lunchroom?"

"Nope. Haven't seen him yet."

Shannon checked her watch. Most days they arrived about the same time. Today she'd come in a few minutes early to be sure she could read the Secret Admirer's note in private. With the clock now showing ten minutes after Todd's usual arrival time, a niggling worry started to prod Shannon. She rose and unlocked the filing cabinet so she could get his phone number out of his personnel file; but just as she touched the folder with his name on it, the familiar sound of Todd's laughter echoed from the dispatch office.

With a quick push, she closed the drawer and engaged the locking button, then walked to the dispatch office. She found Todd and one of the drivers in the small room, talking with someone she'd never seen before through the window opening into the drivers' area. Bryan, Rick, and Gary were nowhere to be seen.

"Todd? What time did you get here? I wanted to talk to you."

"About what?" When he turned to face her, he was still winding down his laughter. His eyes were moist, and he swiped over them with his sleeve. "Did you need a form for Terry? He's been here once before, about four months ago, Gary says."

"No, it isn't that. I just wanted to remind you about what

we talked about yesterday."

He grinned, and Faye's words echoed through Shannon's head. Todd truly was even more handsome when he smiled. In the throes of his laughter, his smile was almost magnetic. It was the same smile she remembered from her high school days, when she briefly had a mad crush on him; only now the years and alleged maturity added attractive little crow's feet to the corners of his big, brown eyes. "I haven't forgotten. I'll keep my ears open and let you know if something comes up." With the other men standing behind Todd, neither one could see his face. Using that advantage, Todd placed his hand over his heart and gave her an exaggerated wink. "Promise."

Shannon opened her mouth, but no words came out. Her heart started pounding, just as it had back in those foolish high school days.

Before she said something stupid, Shannon spun around and strode out of the room. She busied herself with her work, ignoring all around her until Faye appeared at the front of her desk to announce it was time for coffee break.

They had barely sat down before Faye started talking. "Have you been in the dispatch area today? It's nuts in there."

Shannon nodded. "I know. Where's Gary? He should be in there with both Rick and Bryan off."

"Gary had a bunch of meetings lined up this morning, and he couldn't cancel. Todd seems to be doing okay in there, considering."

"I noticed you checked on him fairly often."

Faye smiled. "Yeah. I got him coffee a couple of times. I thought he could use it. He said he really appreciated it."

Shannon sighed. "You've got it bad. Maybe there's medication for that."

Faye grinned. "Get serious, Shan. Todd's different from anyone else I've ever met."

Shannon nearly choked on her tea. "You can say that again."

Faye's smile disappeared. "I don't know what you have against him."

Shannon looked down into her mug, not able to face Faye as she spoke. "I already told you Todd is my brother's friend. Let's just say we haven't always gotten along that great over the years. I guess I'm finding it a bit strange to see him so normal, for lack of a better word. I can't help but expect this is a bad dream and I'm waiting for the punch line. Any moment, I feel as if I'm going to wake up, and he'll do something to embarrass or insult me the way he did when we were kids. I know I shouldn't feel that way. After all, it's been over a month now, and he's been nice to me and everything's been fine."

In fact, things were more than fine, even outside of work when no one was around he'd have to answer to or see the next day. When the bookstore closed, she'd enjoyed their time together so much that for a moment she'd wished the store was open until midnight, just so she could have stayed to talk with Todd longer.

Faye smiled dreamily. "Yeah. He's mighty fine."

Shannon rolled her eyes. "Oh, puh-leeze."

"I can dream, can't I?"

"He's not some movie star or idol in one of those teen magazines. He's just Todd."

"If you've known him for years, haven't you ever thought of what it would be like if something developed between you?"

Briefly, when she was going through a period of teenage insanity. She wondered if Faye had heard a word she just said about how sometimes she didn't know whether to scream or cry after yet another unpleasant day spent with Todd and her brother. Before she could answer, Faye continued her questioning.

"Haven't you ever considered what it would be like to be alone with him, like on a romantic date?"

Actually, she had been alone with him prior to last night,

but it wasn't on a date. Craig and Todd were in the garage at her parents' home. She'd gone to tell Craig their mother wanted him for something, so Craig went into the house, leaving her alone in the garage with Todd for a few minutes. For entertainment, Todd asked her to hold some kind of auto part she hadn't known was greasy until it was too late. It took ten solid minutes of scrubbing to get the slime and oily stink off her hands, then a whole day to get the grime out from under her fingernails.

She set her empty mug down on the table with a thud. "I'm sorry, Faye, but I have enough problems with men without adding Todd to the mix."

Faye's eyebrows quirked. "Oh? Is there something you're not telling me?" She leaned closer over the top of the table. "Is it someone here? What's happening? Did you find out who gave you the chocolate kiss? I couldn't find who was giving them out. In fact, no one knew anything about chocolate kisses."

Shannon sucked in a deep breath. "Oh, Faye. . .you didn't go around asking, did you?"

"I asked a couple of people where they came from, but not many. Why?"

"Because it was just meant for me. There was a note attached." Shannon leaned toward Faye, then straightened, not wanting anyone to see they obviously wanted to keep their conversation confidential, as that would attract attention. "I'm afraid I have a Secret Admirer."

Faye's eyes widened. "Wow! That's so exciting!"

"Shh!" Shannon fanned one hand in the air, then hunched in the chair. "Don't tell anyone. I have no idea who it could be. Think. If you were asking around about the chocolate kiss, then that makes at least a couple of people I can eliminate from my list. Who did you talk to?"

"Nanci and Brenda."

Shannon's heart sank.

"Sorry. I didn't ask any of the guys. I didn't think any of them would be bringing stuff like that to work. That's why I just asked women. I didn't specifically say you had one. I just walked up to them and asked if they had chocolate, and both said no."

"I guess that's okay then. Whoever he is, he has to know I'm trying to figure it out. I just don't want him to think I have an investigative team out looking for him, or he'll stop doing it, then I'll never know." She didn't want to tell Faye that Todd was already helping her. From past experience, she knew Todd could be very tight-lipped when it suited him. No one would ever know Todd knew about the Secret Admirer or that he was helping her discover the man's identity.

Faye, on the other hand, was not known for being discreet.

"Just keep your ears and eyes open, but please don't say anything to anyone, and especially don't ask questions. If you hear something, tell me, and I'll take it from there, okay?"

Faye nodded, the personification of seriousness. "Okay."

Shannon pushed the chair back and stood. "We had better get back to work. I have a million things to do."

Shannon couldn't stop thinking about Todd, even though she didn't see him. His absence in the lunchroom during break times only served to show she'd come to expect his presence. He was buried in work, dealing with a system he wasn't entirely proficient at yet, while doing the volume of at least two people. He only came out of the dispatch office a couple of times, when he ran for the washroom, then right back.

By the time Gary finally returned, it was half an hour before quitting time. Bill left the room, but she still didn't see Todd.

When it was time to go home for the day, Shannon hadn't completed all she'd wanted to do to meet her payroll dead-line for the next day. Rather than leave it for the last minute, she took advantage of the quiet office to work undisturbed.

Twenty minutes after everyone else left, Todd emerged from the dispatch room at a slow pace, the wear and tear of a stress-filled day apparent on his face and in his posture.

She couldn't help but feel sorry for him.

"Hey, Todd. How did things go in there?"

"Okay, I guess, but I can't remember ever being so tired." He turned and looked at Faye's empty desk. He pulled her chair out and sank down into it. "Since it's just you and me here, do you mind if I talk to you about something?"

Shannon had a feeling she knew what he was going to say. She'd seen Faye going in and out of the dispatch office a number of times, sometimes with Todd's coffee mug in her hand; other times, Faye was empty-handed. Shannon didn't mind helping him out or giving him a bit of womanly perspective, but she didn't want to do it in the middle of the office. Even though the other regular day staff had left, Gary was still in his office and could appear at any time. Also, not all the drivers were in, and the afternoon-shift warehouse staff members were just beginning their day. Any one of them could walk in at any time, and often did, once they realized she was still there.

Shannon stood. "I have a better idea. You look so tired. Let's go to my place. I just happen to have a great lasagna left over in the fridge from yesterday. All I have to do is heat it up and make a salad, and we'll have a ready-made dinner. We can talk then, without any worry about being disturbed."

"You're inviting me over to your place? And you're also going to feed me?"

"I guess. I just thought it would be a better place to talk."

"That sounds great. I appreciate it."

"I only have to finish what I'm doing."

Todd lounged in Faye's chair until Shannon was ready, then followed her out and into the parking lot. Shannon unlocked her car door but didn't get in. Instead, she stood watching Todd, who was standing beside his car and pressing his hands to every pocket in his jacket, jeans, then shirt.

"I don't believe this," he called out. "I must have forgotten my car keys in the office. I'll be right back, unless Gary sees me. Don't leave without me, because I've never been to your place before. I'm not exactly sure where it is."

"No problem."

As Todd jogged back into the building, Shannon had time to think about what she'd just done.

Surely, she was losing her mind. She'd just invited Todd Sanders to her apartment. The apartment she moved into so she could get away from him.

That she felt sorry for him further confirmed she was losing her mind. She justified it by telling herself she was doing it to talk to him for Faye's benefit and was making the sacrifice for a friend.

Todd was back within minutes, and she was soon on her way, with him following. She pointed him to the visitor parking area, then entered the residents' underground parking area. She was about to push the button in the elevator when she realized she'd left Todd outside. Not only did he not have a key to get in, but he didn't know which was her apartment, although he certainly could find it from the listing by the door.

Instead of hitting the button for the fifth floor, Shannon rode the elevator to the lobby, where she walked to the main door to let Todd in, then took him to her apartment.

"This seems like a nice place. You like living here?"

"Yes. For an apartment, it's pretty peaceful."

Having known him for years, she was comfortable with Todd's help in getting their dinner together. They only chatted about inconsequential things until it was ready and on the table.

For a second, Shannon hesitated. Even when she was alone, which was most of the time, she always bowed her head and gave God thanks for her meal and her day. She didn't know if Todd did the same.

She'd seen him in church, and Craig had told her about Todd's turning his life over to Jesus. She'd also seen him in action at work. All these showed a man living his faith. But this was the first time she was alone with Todd in a private setting. No one was there with him except her, and God, of course.

After knowing Todd for so long, there was no pretense between them. Sometimes she felt that Todd didn't consider her any differently than an annoying piece of furniture. He never pretended to be anything he was not, and he never changed his behavior because she was there. She'd seen him happy and sad. She'd seen him at his best, and definitely at his worst.

Todd smiled at her, clasped his hands, bowed his head, and waited for a few seconds for her to do the same. "Dear heavenly Father, thank You for the food we're about to eat. Thank You for Shannon and her willingness to open her home and share it with me. Thanks, too, for the good jobs You've given both of us, and I pray we'll be able to show Your glory to all who work there. Amen!"

"Amen," Shannon murmured, unable to believe the tightness that formed in her throat from his heartfelt words.

Todd didn't wait for her to respond or start talking. He began eating right away. "This is great," he said, speaking through his mouthful. "I didn't realize how hungry I was until we started heating this up. I didn't have time to stop for lunch. All I've had today was a bag of chips out of the machine and a few dozen cups of coffee."

Shannon cleared her throat and reached for the salad dressing. "Yes, I had a feeling."

After a few more hearty mouthfuls, Todd slowed down. "Actually, that's what I have to talk to you about."

"You want to talk to me about your bad eating habits?"

He sighed while he rose and helped himself to another piece of lasagna from the pan. "No. About Faye and the coffee. She came in more times than I could count to bring me coffee. While I appreciated it, I think it's getting out of hand."

"You admit you've been drinking too much coffee?"

He sat down at the table with his refilled plate but didn't continue eating. "Get serious, Shan. I think I'm starting to see what it's like when I did this kind of thing to you, and I'm sorry I used to do that. I wanted to talk to you about Faye."

Shannon nodded. Of course she'd known what he was going to say. She'd already heard Faye's side of the story. Faye had made her feelings toward Todd rather obvious. Shannon knew him well enough to realize that if he returned her feelings, even in the slightest, he would already have asked her out. Still, she had to give him a chance to say the reason he was seeking her out. "Sorry. I didn't mean to be like that. What did you want to ask me?"

"I don't know what to do about Faye."

"You know she likes you."

"I know that. I think everyone in the office knows. And probably half the drivers, too."

"Why don't you take her out a few times and see what happens? Faye is really nice. After awhile, it'll either work, or it won't."

"It wouldn't be right to do that. I'm old enough now that I have to be realistic. Any relationship I enter into could develop into marriage, and I can't marry Faye. I don't know her that well, but I don't think she's a believer. I don't want to get into something like that."

Shannon nodded. "I know what you mean. But I think Faye is a Christian. She's even been to church with me a couple of times. I get the impression that something in the church has hurt her, and she's stepped back. She doesn't want to talk about it, but I think she just needs some time to work things out, and she'll be fine."

"I can understand her situation, but that doesn't change the way I feel. I have to figure out a way to tell her gently I'm not interested. It wouldn't be fair to go out with her when I know nothing would come of it."

"You don't know that."

"But I *do* know that." Todd raised his fork in the air with his right hand and placed his left hand over his chest. "Because my heart already belongs to someone else."

Shannon nearly choked on her food. Despite how ridiculous he looked, she knew he was serious. Todd may have been a lot of things, but he had never been a liar. The more she was getting to know the new Todd, the more she knew he wasn't a liar now. "I didn't know. Aren't you going to tell me about it?"

With his hand still over his heart, Todd shook his head. "Nope. It's a secret."

"I think there are too many secrets around here," Shannon grumbled as she stuffed the last bite of lasagna into her mouth. First she had a Secret Admirer, and now Todd had secrets, too. All those secrets were going to drive her insane.

Todd settled back into position and began eating again. "By the way, Craig tells me you're coming to the open house at church on Saturday."

"Yes, I am. Are you going?"

He grinned. "Wouldn't miss it for the world."

seven

Todd straightened his tie, fixed the knot, and stood back to look at himself in the mirror, trying to get some satisfaction from his pristine appearance.

He yanked off the tie. It was his face, but he wasn't the man in the mirror.

The man in the mirror was dressed up in a neatly ironed shirt and black dress slacks, now minus the perfectly matched tie. He had just had a haircut and was freshly shaved.

He didn't know why he was trying so hard. Nothing he changed on the outside was going to make a difference to Shannon. She was never swayed by outward appearances. When she looked at him, she saw only a man who used to taunt and tease her when she was dressed up in her finest to go on a date. A man who frequently rummaged through her parents' refrigerator and ate the leftovers she had intended to take for her lunch at work. A man who made rude remarks to her in any situation.

In her position, he wouldn't have liked that guy, either.

He had to make up for every ignorant and stupid thing he'd ever done to her, and clothing and a haircut weren't going to do it. More than anything, he wanted to tell her how sorry he was, but he'd learned the hard way that talk was cheap.

Todd covered his face with his hands. "Lord God, I don't know what to do," he mumbled between his fingers. A million thoughts roared through his mind, none of which would be helpful.

He walked into the kitchen to sit at the table where he had the rhyming dictionary, a pen, and a piece of paper handy.

Soon he had to leave for church, but he had enough time to write down his thoughts.

> Dearest Shannon,
>> My heart longs for the day we can be together
>> In either fine or stormy weather.
>> In every way it's you I adore,
>> Because every day I love you more.
>>> Your Secret Admirer

Without analyzing his words, Todd rolled the note, tied it with a ribbon, and attached a chocolate kiss. He'd already left the note she would find Monday, but this one he would leave for her Tuesday.

He didn't know if she could ever love him as much as he loved her, but so far, the fact that she was tolerating him gave him hope. He hadn't considered how he'd feel about writing the notes every day, but it made him feel good to know she appeared to enjoy reading them. But there was a benefit he hadn't thought of. Not that he would ever regard himself as the creative or artistic type, but pouring out his heart onto paper, even if she didn't know who was creating the words, was therapeutic. Since he couldn't tell her in person how he felt, writing the notes was the next best thing.

Never in his life had Todd waxed poetic, but now he was doing so—literally. He found it ironic, since back in high school he'd passed English only by the grace of his teachers.

On his drive to church, he tried to compose more verses in his head. He wasn't having much success, except he knew what he wanted to say. For the actual writing of the words, the rhyming dictionary was probably the best purchase he'd ever made.

The parking lot was nearly full when he pulled in. The spot he found was farther from the building than ever before, giving him a slightly different perspective of the building and grounds from the usual.

The church wasn't big or grand, but the building was solid and well cared for. Since the board had been preparing for the anniversary celebration for months, some of the church's history had crept into the Sunday sermons. He'd learned the building had been constructed a year after the church was planted twenty-five years ago, due to the generosity of the parent church and a member of the missions conference. Even though he'd attended for only a year and a half, he knew both Craig and Shannon had grown up there, attending almost every Sunday. Everyone knew the Andrews family and loved them.

In comparing his own home life to theirs, he'd seen what he'd missed by not growing up in a stable environment. After experiencing the added love of extended family through other church members, he missed even more not having a network of people and programs to fall back on when he needed them. For a few years, however, that had been his own fault. Ever since he met Craig, Craig had given him an open invitation to go to church or even church activities if he didn't want to attend Sunday morning, which he hadn't. Todd had rejected Craig's offers of help, telling himself he could handle his life on his own. In so many ways, he'd been a fool. Ever since he had experienced the grace of God's love, he joined in freely, although for now the best he could do was help Craig supervise and provide transportation for the youth group's activities. He bit back a wry smile, thinking that most of the kids knew the Bible better than he did. But he was working on it, and Craig assured him that was what mattered.

As he walked closer to the building, he recognized Shannon's car. Judging from her good parking spot, close to the building, she'd arrived much sooner than he had.

Fortunately, the weather was warm for an early spring day. The committee had been prepared for rain, but the weather was cooperating, ensuring the Saturday open house would be a success. The aroma of the barbecue already enticed him before he reached the crowd milling on the grass. The people gathered outside already exceeded the usual number present for a normal Sunday service. Judging from the cars, which were being parked on the street, the people inside would be almost equal to those outside.

He only waved a friendly greeting at Craig and Shannon's parents in passing, since he saw them every Sunday and a few days during the week, and continued on his quest to find Shannon. He found her with Craig, talking to some people he already knew, making it easy to slip in beside her and not raise any eyebrows.

After sharing a few comments about the number of people present, the conversation continued as it had prior to his arrival. Instead of joking around as he usually did with those same people, Todd kept silent. He listened and watched everyone else.

As conversation continued, each one of them occasionally glanced at him, probably wondering why he wasn't making jokes. Either that or they didn't recognize him since he was all dressed up.

Craig looked at him frequently, but Shannon didn't look at him at all. He had a feeling she was waiting for him to tease her about something and embarrass her in front of their mutual friends. It made him more aware of what a jerk he'd been to her in the past. It had been a year since the last time they'd been in church together, with the exception of a few weeks ago, when he'd tried to be with her and she'd pointedly ignored him. Before that, though, he'd embarrassed her often enough that she would have no reason now to think things had changed.

After the threads of talk about the anniversary celebration were exhausted, Brittany turned to Todd. She then looked at

Shannon and back to Todd, as if she couldn't decide which one of them to speak to.

She turned again to Shannon. "I couldn't believe it when I heard you two were actually working together. How's it going?"

Shannon drew in a short breath. "Fine."

A silence hung in the air within their circle, while Brittany waited for Shannon to say more, but she didn't. Brittany turned to face Todd. Since she appeared to be waiting for something, Todd thought he should answer, even though he considered her question intrusive.

"It's been fine, although we don't see each other all that much. It's a very busy place."

Brittany turned back to Shannon with one eyebrow raised.

Shannon nodded. "It's the same building, but we work in different areas."

Brittany's eyes widened. "Surely you must bump into each other sometime. What about your breaks?"

All eyes remained fixed on them. Todd felt strange with everyone staring at them. He was accustomed to being the center of attention, but this time, he wasn't trying to entertain. Instead, he felt like a bug under a microscope. And to have Shannon under the microscope with him made him angry.

He stiffened from head to toe. "I take my first coffee break at 10:15, my lunch at 12:30, then my second coffee break around 3:00, if I have time. Would you like to know Shannon's schedule, too? Is there anything else you want to know?"

Brittany's face turned beet red. "Sorry. I was just curious because you and Shannon always, uh, never mind—I think I'm going to get a hamburger."

Everyone else mumbled their agreement under their breath, and the group broke up. They headed outside, including Craig, which left Todd as alone with Shannon as he could be in a crowd of people.

He rammed his hands into his pockets. He knew he'd been

relentless at times with Shannon, using her as an easy target. She'd always been so graceful to put up with him that he hadn't considered what everyone else around them saw. He hadn't realized he'd been so bad that everyone would want to know how they could function in the same room together. "I didn't know we were going to be such a topic of interest. This is my fault for teasing you all the time. I'm really sorry."

She tipped her head down, studying some spot on the floor as she spoke. "It's okay. I'm a big girl now. I can handle it."

His heart hammered in his chest. "You shouldn't have to handle it. I wish I could take it all back, but I can't. Saying I'm sorry somehow isn't enough."

She still wouldn't look up at him. "It's okay. I know you weren't that way on purpose. I guess everyone else who didn't know you as well as I did thought we were fighting all the time."

Todd's stomach flipped over. The last thing he wanted to do was fight with Shannon, but he had openly taken out his frustrations on her. Guilt roared through him. He knew he should say something, but he didn't know what. The words spilled out of his mouth before he could think about what he was saying or stop himself. "I don't want to fight with you, Shan. But if it looked as if we were fighting, then we can always kiss and make up."

Her head snapped up, and she stared straight into his eyes. All he could do was grin like an idiot.

"Get real, Todd. Honestly—sometimes I just don't know what goes on inside your brain."

He lost the grin and shrugged his shoulders. "If you won't kiss me, then how about if I get us a couple of burgers?"

"I'll get my own," she muttered.

She turned and walked away, but Todd caught up quickly and walked beside her to the barbecue then stood directly behind her in the line.

"Are you coming back tomorrow for the service?"

She didn't look at him as she replied. "Yes, I had planned on it."

"Are you staying for the speeches and stuff tonight?"

"Yes. Actually, I've been asked to say a few words, since I was the first baby born and dedicated here. In a way I'm almost dreading it, because lots of people here still remember that. I'm going to hear choruses of 'I can't believe how you've grown up' for the next year, I think."

Todd smiled. He also could say how much she'd grown up. The age difference of three years was nothing now, but he remembered what she was like when he first became friends with Craig. One reason he'd paid so much attention to Shannon then was because he was jealous that Craig had a little sister who loved and adored him, while Todd had felt alone.

He touched Shannon's arm gently with one finger, then ran his finger up to her shoulder. While he cupped her shoulder, he rubbed soothing little circles into her shoulder blade with his thumb, as he knew she liked. He dropped his voice to a low whisper so only Shannon could hear him. To further ensure he wouldn't be overheard, he leaned closer to her so his mouth was nearly at her ear. "I can tell you how much you've grown up, but then you could say the same about me, since we met when we were both kids. I won't talk if you don't."

A few strands of her hair tickled his nose, but Todd didn't move. He'd never been so close to Shannon, touching her gently, when she wasn't backing away or screaming because he was tickling or poking her with something. His eyes drifted shut as he blocked out the smell of the meat on the grill and inhaled the heady aroma of her apple-scented shampoo.

"Todd?"

He nuzzled in closer. "Mmm. . .you smell so nice."

Suddenly, she stepped forward. Even though the spring air was warm, the abrupt separation felt like an arctic front had fallen between them. "What are you doing? What's gotten into you?"

He felt his ears heat up as he became aware of their surroundings and the people around them, even though no one was looking at them. "Sorry. Is it almost our turn?"

As they filled their plates and found a place to sit and eat, Todd kept the conversation light. The closer they came to the start of the evening service, the more nervous Shannon became. Fortunately, it was easy for Todd to slip into his old behavior patterns. He made jokes and wisecracks and soon had her laughing, and with her laughter time passed quickly.

When the service began, he had convinced her everyone else who had been called on to speak was as nervous as she was. They listened to other people tell their stories of being with the church body in the last twenty-five years, some giving testimonies and some history lessons on the church's founding. Others talked of the transition from a home group to constructing and moving into a dedicated building. Most people simply shared times that were special to them.

Todd had never thought of what Shannon would be like in front of a large group; but once she overcame her fear of the microphone, she was a good speaker—clear, easy to understand, and entertaining. By the time she finished her short speech on growing up from birth to adulthood in the same congregation, he heard a few elderly ladies sniffling, none of whom was Shannon's grandmother.

"You were great," he said as she returned to her seat and shuffled in beside him.

"Thanks." Joy radiated from Shannon as she smiled ear to ear. It made Todd hope that one day she would smile like that for him.

They sat quietly for the rest of the service. At the close, everyone stood and joined with the choir in a rousing rendition of the "Hallelujah Chorus."

They talked with several people as they all made their way out of the building.

When one of the elderly ladies who had been sniffling in the back row stopped Shannon at the door, Todd said good-bye and walked out to the parking lot to his car.

As he pointed the key toward the lock, he paused. Something felt wrong—as if he were too high.

He looked at the front tire. It was completely flat and sitting on the rim. The back tire was the same. He noticed that the car beside his had a flattened tire as well, but at least it was only one. Todd walked around to the other side of his car. Fortunately, that side was untouched.

He sucked in a deep breath and checked inside, making sure his stereo was still intact, which it was.

He walked back to the driver's side and rested his fists on his hips. He couldn't tell if someone had let the air out of the tires or if the tires had been punctured. He certainly wasn't going to have the car towed, if all he had to do was reinflate the tires. He had a spare, but with two tires flattened, one spare wouldn't do him a lot of good.

A few unkind words tumbled through his mind, but he stopped himself before he said them out loud. He returned to the church, where he found Shannon still talking to the same lady. She looked as if she wanted to get away, and fortunately, Todd could help her.

"Excuse me, Shan—may I talk to you? There's something wrong with my car."

The lady, whose name he couldn't remember, waved her hand, smiled, and walked away to stop some other people who also looked as if they were trying to leave.

"What's wrong? Or were you just being a hero and rescuing me?"

He ran his fingers through his hair. "I wish I were being gallant, but it looks as if someone let the air out of a couple of my tires. I have a portable compressor, but it's at home. Can you give me a ride? You have to go sort of past my place anyway."

"Someone flattened your tires!?" She raised her hands to cover her mouth. "Here? At church?"

"It's a sick world we live in, Shan. Nothing is safe." That was an early lesson he learned. Nowhere was a safe haven, not even home, which should have been one of the first places a person could go.

"Of course I'll give you a ride home. Let's go."

He followed Shannon to her car, and soon, they were on the way to his apartment.

"I really appreciate this. Would you mind picking me up on the way to church, too? I can leave the car in the lot overnight and then pump the tires back up after the service is over."

"No problem. But if you want to go back and do it now, I don't mind. It's still earl—"

Shannon gasped and slammed on the brakes. The tires screeched. Todd lurched forward but avoided smacking his face into the windshield only by the seatbelt locking and holding him in place. The car jerked with the bump of a small impact. A big black dog bounced slightly off the front right fender and landed on the road beside the car. Before Todd could think of what to do, the dog scrambled up and bounded away.

"I hit him," Shannon whimpered. "I just hit a dog."

Todd watched the dog disappear between a couple of houses. "Yeah, but he couldn't be hurt too bad. He's running away."

A horn honked behind them. Shannon started moving forward but far below the speed limit.

He turned toward her. All the color had drained from her face. She was gripping the steering wheel so tight her knuckles had turned white. Even from the side, he could see her eyes were glassy.

"Maybe you should pull over."

She shook her head. "I can't. There's nowhere to stop here."

"We're only a few blocks from my place. Maybe you should come inside with me and settle down a bit before you go home."

She nodded tightly. "Maybe I will."

He directed her to the visitor parking, since the control for the underground security parking area was still attached to the visor of his own car.

"I'm sure the dog is okay," he said as he punched in the code to open the front door. "After all, it ran away. But I know it's a shock to hit something. I once hit a deer when I was in the mountains. It was pretty scary. The deer ran away, too, but I had to pull over for awhile."

All she did was nod.

Todd guided her up the elevator and to his apartment. Once inside, he left her at the door and hurried into the kitchen ahead of her. He picked up the rhyming dictionary from the table and shoved it into the nearest drawer. Shannon appeared behind him just as he opened the cupboard above the stove. After he started working at Kwiki Kouriers, he'd bought a box of Shannon's favorite tea in the faint hope that one day she would come for a visit. He was happy to have it on hand, although these weren't the circumstances under which he had wanted to give it to her.

He started pouring water into the kettle. "If you want, I can ask around the neighborhood and see if anyone knows who owns the dog and maybe check up on it for you."

Shannon's voice wavered as she spoke. "Yes, that would be nice." Her lower lip quivered. Tears started to stream down her cheeks. Todd set the kettle aside, took a few steps toward her, and extended his arms. "Come here," he said softly.

Without saying a word, Shannon stepped into the cradle of his arms. As he closed his arms around her, she cried even more. Her whole body shook.

"It's okay," he murmured as he stroked her hair with one hand. "He didn't appear to be limping. I watched him run away." Despite his words, he knew that as soon as Shannon left, he was going to take a flashlight and walk to the spot and check to make sure there was no blood. Only then would he be satisfied the dog probably wasn't seriously hurt, but he wasn't going to tell her that until after he'd confirmed it.

After a few minutes, she stopped crying, but Todd didn't let her go. Since she made no effort to move away from him, he kept his arms around her, holding her close to his heart.

In the car, he had considered hinting to her that he was the writer of the notes. He'd been praying for a sign to show him when the time was right to tell her he was her Secret Admirer. Even though he didn't appreciate the flat tires, it did create a situation he could have used to his advantage.

That had now changed, though. He couldn't tell her he loved her when she was so upset over hitting a dog. But, in holding her, he was more certain he wanted to do this forever. He wanted to be there for Shannon when she needed someone. He wanted her trust, and he wanted her to know he would do anything for her.

With her leaning into his hug with no hesitation, he wanted to know the same thing could happen again, only next time not in trying circumstances. He wanted to be able to hold her in good times and in bad. In sickness and in health, until death parted them.

He loved her so much he wanted to marry her.

But he couldn't ask her such a thing yet. He didn't know how she would respond when he told her he was her Secret Admirer.

She shuffled in his arms but didn't back up or indicate she wanted him to release her. Her words sounded muffled as she spoke against his chest. In a way, he liked the vibration of her voice against him. It was a tangible reminder of how close she was and that she wasn't backing away. "I'm so sorry for acting like such a ninny and crying like that. I know the dog ran away, but I couldn't stop myself."

Todd lowered his head so his cheek pressed against her temple. Her skin was soft, and her hair smelled almost as good as it had earlier. He meant to speak clearly, but his voice came out in only a hoarse croak. "It's okay. Don't worry about it."

Slowly, Todd lowered his head a little more, just enough to brush his lips against the soft skin of her cheek. He could taste the saltiness of her tears against his lips.

The sensation drove him over the edge. He couldn't stop himself. Or rather, he probably could have stopped, but he didn't want to. Ever so gently, he brushed a light kiss on her cheek in that spot. He brushed another soft kiss a little farther down, closer to her mouth. When she sighed, he stopped. His cheek was against hers, and their lips so close he could almost taste her. In slow motion, Todd slid one hand up her back then over her shoulders, until he touched her chin with the tip of his index finger. He guided her chin up, closed his eyes, and kissed her mouth—lightly, gently, and only for a second.

His heart raced. He wanted to kiss her again, only longer and fully.

Again, he guided her chin with his finger, just to tip her chin up a little more.

Suddenly, Shannon stiffened and stepped backward.

Todd let his arms drop. He would never hold her against her will. He knew she would never have expected him to kiss her, but he hadn't thought about her reaction until it happened. All he knew was that he wanted to do it again and do it right—he wanted to kiss her well and good, only stopping for breath long enough to tell her he loved her and to hear she loved him, too.

"I think I should go. I'll see you tomorrow morning. 'Bye."

The door closed before he had a chance to say a word.

eight

Shannon set her mug on the corner of her desk, then slid into her chair. She grasped the handle of her drawer but didn't open it.

If the Secret Admirer wasn't perplexing enough, now she had Todd to think about, too.

Todd.

Because she was at work, Shannon fought the urge to cover her face with her hands.

Again Todd Sanders was driving her insane.

When she picked him up for church Sunday morning, it was as if everything were normal, but things would never be normal again. Actually, where Todd was concerned, she didn't know what normal was.

He'd been his usual bright, cheery self on the way to church. When they arrived, he tossed a black case into the trunk of his car, and they went into the service together. To be safe, she'd immediately gone to sit with her parents. Taking it for granted he was welcome, Todd had followed right along with her, and they'd all sat together.

To make matters worse, her parents invited her for lunch at the close of the service. After she accepted, they also invited Todd. Of course, he accepted, too.

The last time she'd stayed for a meal at her parents' house when Todd was present had been two years ago, before she moved out. Todd and Craig had been in rare form that day. They'd been out fishing together, and neither of them had taken a shower before coming to the table. The stench of sweaty men, fish, and diesel fuel turned her stomach so bad she asked them to move and sit near an open window.

Neither Todd nor Craig moved, but Todd teased her relentlessly for making the request.

Then, while they were eating, Todd expressed his frustration to her mother about the problems he had gutting the fish he'd caught that morning, including a detailed portrayal of the procedure he'd used. Her mother had listened intently, giving Todd some suggestions on how to get a clean cut next time, including another vivid description of the various body parts of a dead fish, while Shannon struggled to keep her stomach settled.

The final straw came when Todd pulled some kind of huge dead bug out of his pocket, claiming he was going to make a fishing lure to look exactly like it.

Everyone had thought he was funny. Except Shannon. She thought he'd been rude and obnoxious, which was typical for Todd.

On Sunday, he'd been so polite and well mannered the whole day, she wouldn't have known he was the same man. Since she hadn't known what to do or say, she'd said little and listened to Todd talk. Even if he wasn't a scholar, he had certainly been a gentleman.

Something was wrong, but she couldn't figure out what.

At the sound of a thud echoing from the lunchroom, Shannon returned her thoughts to where she was and opened the drawer. She pulled out the note of the day, but instead of reading it, she held it in her hand.

So far she could handle the Secret Admirer. The notes were flattering and sweet, even sensitive and kind. No one had ever told her she was special before, and especially not in such an old-fashioned and romantic manner. If she allowed herself the fantasy, she could have called the writing love sonnets, rather than bad poetry. She was enjoying the attention and anticipated coming to work so she could read the new note.

She grasped the end of the ribbon, about to tug it open, when Todd's laughter rang out from the lunchroom.

Her hand froze, and she shut her eyes.

Todd.

He'd been so sweet to her Saturday night that it seemed almost natural when he kissed her.

Shannon had to force herself to breathe. Todd Sanders had kissed her.

He'd kissed her once before. She'd been seventeen, and it had been the day of her high school graduation. When she arrived home from the ceremony, diploma in hand, ready to change for the dinner celebration, she'd found Todd and Craig in the living room. Todd had smiled and held his arms open, and she'd gone to him with stars in her eyes. When he asked if he could give her a celebratory kiss, she thought she had died and gone to heaven. Just like a schoolgirl, which of course she was at the time, her heart pounded out of control, and she could barely breathe as he bent down. His lips brushed her ear, setting her all a-quiver. Then he whispered "woof" in her ear and licked up the side of her face. He was across the room before she could lift her arm fast enough to smack him.

But on Saturday, when he kissed her so gently and sweetly, she'd stood very still. She had even wanted him to kiss her again. He'd definitely improved on his kissing skills, which wasn't what she should have been thinking about.

Surely she was going insane.

Just as she had told Todd before, she was a big girl now. And Todd was now a grown man. He'd been a great comfort to her and done the right things while she cried so much after the shock of hitting the dog, who may not have been hurt after all. She supposed she'd even made it easy for him. Any man in that situation probably would have done the same.

But this wasn't any man. It was Todd Sanders. She shouldn't have wanted more.

So she'd acted like the grown-up woman she was. She ran

away. And now she was simply going to pretend it hadn't happened.

"Hey, Shan. Top 'o the morning to ya," Todd quipped in a bad, fake Irish accent as he passed by, coffee in hand, before he disappeared into the dispatch office.

Behind him, Faye giggled.

Shannon gagged.

When Todd disappeared from sight, Faye sighed. "Are you coming tonight? I have a seat reserved for you."

"Tonight?"

"Did you forget? We're all going out for Rick's birthday. To that steak place a few blocks away."

"I remember, now that you mention it. Yes, of course I'm going."

Faye nodded and sat down at her desk. Shannon didn't want to think about the fact that Todd might go, but she wouldn't stay away just because he would be there. She refused to let him control her life, even if it was in an indirect way.

For now, Shannon wanted to read the newest note. Faye already knew about them, and so did Todd, but he didn't count. She'd waited too long, though, and other staff had started to arrive in the office. She didn't want to wait until the end of the day when the office would once again be empty, so she picked up the note, shoved it into her pocket, and ran into the washroom.

She tried to tell herself that reading it in the washroom didn't lessen the romanticism of the situation.

Dearest Shannon,
    Again I am glad the weekend is finished
    Because my love for you has not diminished.
    Monday has come, and I get to see you once more
    And tuck another note and a kiss in your drawer.
                                   Your Secret Admirer

Shannon smiled as she reread the note. The poetry might be getting worse, but the words still warmed her heart. She popped the kiss into her mouth, savoring it until the last morsel had dissolved, then returned to her desk and began her work for the day.

The whole day, she eagerly anticipated the coming dinner, not that the occasion was extraordinary.

But maybe, just maybe, *He* would be there.

⁊

Todd walked into the dimly lit restaurant. He was with Rick and Bryan, but soon he would be with Shannon.

The atmosphere was happy and informal, just a bunch of people who didn't necessarily know each other well getting together for a fun evening. Since more than twenty-five people were attending, a small room had been reserved for their group. It was a private gathering so everyone would be free to sit down, eat, or mingle as they wished. It would be more of a party atmosphere than a formal dinner gathering, and people could leave early or stay until the restaurant closed.

The scenario was perfect for Todd. If he spent most of his time with Shannon, no one would notice or care.

Shannon stood near the front of the room, talking to Faye. Just as Todd was about to join Shannon, Gary appeared beside Rick.

Without preamble, Rick elbowed Gary in the ribs and made a crude comment about Shannon's figure. Gary responded in like manner. Todd's mouth nearly dropped open in shock, but he struggled to compose himself. What they were saying was nothing he hadn't thought himself before he became a Christian. He'd even said a few of the same things out loud to Shannon years ago. Suddenly, he felt ashamed.

He had an almost uncontrollable urge to go and stand between the men and Shannon, so they wouldn't be able to look at her. Of course, that would provide only a temporary solution. His actions would simply stall their observations and discussion for a short time.

But any time was better than no time.

He turned to Gary. "Excuse me. I just remembered something."

Todd forced himself to walk, not run, as he crossed the room to join Shannon and Faye.

"Good evening, ladies." He smiled first at Faye, then more at Shannon, hoping he wasn't being too obvious. "Mind if I join you?"

Faye wrapped her fingers around his arm. "Please do! We could use some manly company, right, Shan?"

Shannon glanced from side to side, then back to Todd. "I guess."

Todd shuffled a few inches to block Gary's view of Shannon. "This is a great idea. By the way, who's collecting the money?"

Faye stuck out her hand. "Me. This month only Rick is having a birthday, so everyone else pays for just one meal. One dollar, please."

Todd gave her the dollar. For the person or persons having a birthday that month, everyone else contributed enough money to cover their meals. Between so many people, it wasn't a large expense, and everyone always had a good time. This was his first dinner since he'd started, and he'd been looking forward to it.

Todd grinned and leaned closer to Faye, but he still spoke loud enough for Shannon to hear. "My birthday is coming up, you know. My last birthday. I'm going to be twenty-nine forevermore."

Shannon rolled her eyes. "Then we'll only have to pay for one dinner—and no more for the rest of your life. It would serve you right. I think I'm going to sit down. Everyone's here, so we're going to get settled and order soon."

"I have a few more people to collect from. I'll catch you

guys later," Faye said and headed across the room.

Todd followed Shannon to one of the tables and sat beside her. She glanced to the other dispatchers and Gary, then back to Todd. She raised an eyebrow. She didn't say a word, but her question was obvious.

"It's okay if I sit with you, isn't it?" Todd tried to calm his heart from going into overdrive as he asked his next question. "We can be friends, can't we?"

She paused, as if she had to think about it. "Yes, I guess so. It just feels strange, that's all."

His gut clenched. The room was filled with people milling about, but for a limited time, they were alone in their own small corner. It wasn't exactly ideal, but he'd made a bit of progress, and he couldn't let the opportunity lapse. He had too much he wanted to say.

"I can only guess how you feel about sitting with me, and I can't blame you. I know words are inadequate, but I don't know what I can do except say I'm sorry for everything I've done to you." For all the good being sorry did. His mother had been sorry for twenty years. She continued to be sorry, but still nothing had changed except he'd become smarter and wiser, he hoped.

"It's okay, Todd. I've been thinking a lot about stuff lately. It's really okay. Since we've been working together, you've been different. I'm working to put everything behind me."

Once again, her unselfish grace washed over him like a cleansing balm. He'd never felt so unworthy beside another person or so undeserving. And he'd never loved her more. "Shan, I know this is going to sound strange, but would you like to go—"

"Hi, Shannon. Todd." Gary's voice interrupted Todd's words.

Todd gritted his teeth. He was about to ask Shannon if she would go out to dinner with him the next day, just the two of them, so they could talk, like a real date. He wasn't going to tell her how much he cared in the middle of a work-related outing. He wanted to show her, in private, away from the hustle and bustle of anything work or church related.

Gary and Rick pulled out chairs and joined them at their table for four. "I brought the birthday boy."

Todd smiled politely, but the last people he felt like sitting with were Gary and Rick, especially after what he'd heard them say. However, since Shannon had no idea what they'd said behind her back, he had no good reason to suggest they move.

Todd nodded and responded when appropriate as they ordered their food. When they received their meals, he did the same as Shannon and bowed his head in silence for a couple of seconds to give thanks to the Lord. He thanked God first for the meal, then for the reason for being with everyone out in a restaurant—his good job.

To enjoy the evening, Todd pushed the crude comments out of his head. When they finished eating, he stood and mingled, as did everyone else. He wanted to spend every minute he could with Shannon, but he knew it would look strange if he never left her side.

Still, the second dessert tray arrived, he made a beeline for his seat before anyone else could sit beside Shannon. As he knew she would, she selected a slice of triple chocolate cake while he chose a hearty piece of peach pie.

He hadn't finished his first bite when Gary reappeared, this time without Rick, but with a chocolate dessert.

Gary lowered himself into the chair. "I see you also picked chocolate. A woman after my own heart."

Todd stiffened.

Shannon smiled at Gary. "I've had this here before. It's the best I've ever had." She turned back to Todd. "There's one at the bookstore that runs a close second, though."

Gary continued to look solely at Shannon, ignoring Todd.

"That may be so. But nothing beats pure chocolate. Like, for example, a chocolate kiss."

Shannon dropped her fork.

Todd nearly choked at Gary's mention of a chocolate kiss. He'd wondered if Gary had seen the note with the kiss attached the day he went into Shannon's drawer. Now, after hearing his roundabout reference to it, he knew he had.

Gary smiled and leaned slightly closer to Shannon. "I love chocolate, too."

Todd's stomach took a nosedive into his shoes. Unless he was mistaken, Gary had just intimated he was somehow connected to the chocolate kisses Todd had been leaving for Shannon every day.

Todd cleared his throat, hoping his voice would come out sounding casual. "I think most people like chocolate, Gary."

Gary's expression turned smug as he watched Shannon take a shaky sip of her coffee. "Probably. Just some people think chocolate is more special than others. Sometimes it even carries a message."

Shannon started coughing in the middle of her sip. She set the cup down in the saucer so fast she spilled some, while she pressed her other fist into the center of her chest.

Todd narrowed his eyes. Gary was slick; there was no doubt about it. He'd seen hints of that characteristic while working with him. Now he saw the trait extended into Gary's personal life and thoughts as well, which shouldn't have been a surprise.

He opened his mouth to counter, even though he hadn't yet put his thoughts together to make a coherent sentence. Before he could get a word out, Faye slid into the empty chair.

"Hi, Gary. You still owe me a dollar."

Gary leaned sideways in the chair to retrieve his wallet from his back pocket. "Of course. Is everyone having fun?"

Faye nodded. "As always. What about you, Todd? This is your first time."

All he could think about was the new complication to his Secret Admirer plan. Shannon had asked him to listen to the talk around him, to see if he could help her discover who was leaving the kisses. She never actually told him about the notes, and he didn't know if she'd done that on purpose or by simple omission. Even though Gary wouldn't know what was in the notes, it would have been an easy guess. The point was that he knew, and he'd mentioned the kisses to Shannon.

Todd didn't know if Shannon had told any of the other women, but he did know he was the only male she'd confided in. The only reason for that was his unique position in what he could now call, with caution, an old friend.

Being in transition from nemesis to friend wasn't the time to tell Shannon he was her Secret Admirer. Despite her forgiveness, he had to prove himself. He could tell she was still being cautious around him. He had to earn her trust and, if he could, a little affection, before it was time to reveal himself to her.

Gary's sudden appearance in the scenario complicated things. He couldn't tell Shannon that Gary wasn't her Secret Admirer. To know he wasn't, Todd would have to know who was, and he couldn't say so yet.

But just as Shannon didn't know the Secret Admirer was Todd, neither did Gary. He also didn't realize Todd knew there was a Secret Admirer, which probably explained why Gary had the nerve to mention "a message" in front of him.

Todd didn't know what Gary had in mind, but he planned to find out.

He turned to smile at Faye. "I'm having a great time. This is a good way to get to know people away from work."

Faye rested her hand on his arm, and her smile turned sappy. "I'm so glad you feel that way."

Todd patted her hand, while desperately thinking of a way to remove it without being too obvious. He knew Faye had a crush on him. He hoped that, like the other women who had developed a fast crush on him because of his smile and his ability to tell a good joke, her crush would fade as quickly as it started. He didn't want to hurt Faye. He liked her, but only as a friend at work.

He turned toward Faye's plate, which contained a half-eaten piece of cake. "That looks good. I got the peach pie. It tastes good, too."

Faye looked at his dessert then and saw he'd eaten only one bite. She blushed and released his arm. He immediately began to eat, openly savoring every bite. His acting caused everyone at the table to smile, including Shannon, and they all resumed eating their own desserts.

With Faye's arrival, Gary made no more personal references.

Since it was only Monday evening, no one stayed much longer after the desserts were finished. Todd became caught up in a conversation with one of his coworkers, so he stayed longer than he had intended. In so doing, he found himself walking out to the parking lot at the same time as Gary.

"You said before that you've known Shannon for a long time."

Todd stiffened. "Yes. I'm good friends with her brother."

"I know you don't have anything on now, but have you ever gone out with her?"

Todd didn't know what to say. He didn't know Gary well, but he did know he had a reputation as a playboy and was proud of it.

Todd considered the time he'd spent with Shannon at the bookstore the closest thing to a date he'd ever had with her. The way things were going now, it would be the closest he'd get for a long time. "No," he mumbled. "Never did."

Gary jingled his keys in his pocket as they walked. "But

you've known her for a long time, so that's close enough. Tell me what she likes and doesn't like."

A list of Shannon's favorite things flooded his mind. Books, especially Christian romance fiction. Apple-scented shampoo. The emergence of spring. Animals in general, but especially big dogs of no particular heritage. The color green. Classical music with lots of strings. Tall trees.

He shook his head. He had no intention of helping Gary date Shannon. Since he didn't know what Gary expected to hear, he decided to be vague.

"She likes chocolate," he muttered.

"Anything else? I need more. I want to see what progress I can make with her. You can help your boss, can't you?"

Todd nearly tripped over his own feet. He didn't want to think Gary would use his authority to hire and fire to obtain the information he wanted, in something that had nothing to do with work—and everything to do with Todd's heart.

Fortunately, they had arrived at Todd's car, saving him from having to say too much, but Gary stopped beside him.

Todd opened the door and slid in. He reached to close the door, but Gary stepped forward, preventing Todd from moving it without hitting him and forcing him to reply. Todd remained with his arm outstretched, his hand gripping the handle. "Do you have a cat?"

"No, but my sister does. Does she like cats?"

"Not particularly. Focus on that."

"Great. I trust you'll tell me what I need to know?"

"Sure."

Gary stepped back, finally allowing Todd to close the door.

The dinner Todd had paid good money for threatened to surface. He didn't like the position Gary was putting him in with Shannon. He had no intention of helping Gary try to seduce Shannon. But Gary's veiled threat hung over him. He expected him to provide insider information on Shannon.

If Todd didn't need the job so bad, he would have quit right there. But he couldn't do that. Not only did he need the job, but for years, he'd wanted this particular job. Being a city dispatcher was the dream of a lifetime for him. He didn't have enough experience, but Gary told him when he was hired that he would take the chance, hire him anyway, and let him prove himself. So far, he was exceeding expectations, but he hadn't passed his initial three-month probationary period yet.

The job also paid decent money, something else Todd couldn't make light of. Along with supporting himself, he still had to pay off a few of his mother's debts plus a number of ongoing expenses for her.

He couldn't jeopardize the job, or he'd be out on the street. But he refused to let Gary seduce Shannon or be any part of the man's efforts.

Shannon's faith was solid. He knew she wouldn't date someone like Gary. At least, he hoped she wouldn't.

The first thing Todd did when he arrived at home was to go into the kitchen and page through his rhyming dictionary.

Somehow he had to show Shannon that Gary was not the man behind the notes, but he didn't know what to say that wouldn't also show he was the one. For lack of anything to say, Todd simply wrote from his heart.

Dearest Shannon,
Your words are kind, and your thoughts are tender.
My love to you I completely surrender.
When comes the day I can reveal my name
I hope and pray you will feel the same.
                                        Your Secret Admirer

Once he had rolled and tied the note and attached a kiss, Todd changed into his pajamas. It wasn't his bedtime for hours, but he had a lot of praying to do, and he was going to do it in the dark, where he would have no distractions.

Then maybe tomorrow would be a better day.

nine

Shannon read the newest note a third time. Something was different, but she couldn't figure out what. Finally she told herself it was that the pentameter matched this time. She rose, unlocked her filing cabinet, and tucked the note into the newest envelope.

She smiled as she closed the drawer and pushed in the locking button. Rather than leaving the notes where anyone could gain access to them when she wasn't at her desk, she had been storing them in a safe and secure location. She took each envelope home on Friday, then spent a good portion of every Friday night reading the notes, studying them, and trying to figure out who wrote them.

Her smile faded when she realized she was no closer to discovering the identity of the man than when the notes started appearing. Trying to analyze and compare the handwriting had turned up nothing. No one wrote anything by hand anymore. Everything was sent via the company computer, either e-mailed or printed out for everyone to initial if necessary. She'd used a few signatures to eliminate some people, but the signatures weren't enough to determine a match, as most people's didn't correspond with their normal handwriting.

Her only lead was Gary's mention of the chocolate kisses, but his words were by no means conclusive. She'd been working at Kwiki Kouriers enough years with the same people that it was no surprise for someone to know she loved chocolate, especially chocolate that wasn't mixed with caramel or nuts or common fillers. Still, Gary's reference to chocolate kisses had been bugging her for days. She'd prayed about the Secret Admirer more times than she could count. Over the last couple of days, she'd also prayed about Gary, not that he would be the Secret Admirer—she just wanted to know if he was or wasn't. She hadn't received an answer.

A thud echoed from the kitchen, followed by a grumble.

Shannon smiled. Todd arrived his usual ten minutes after she did. His first stop was the lunchroom. He would pour his coffee, then begin his trek through the office toward the dispatch area. At least twice a week, he overfilled his mug, causing him to spill some coffee on the floor. He then had to go back into the lunchroom for a paper towel to wipe up his mess. She had his routine clocked almost to the minute.

This time she stopped him.

"Todd, I need to talk to you."

He smiled so vividly she could see the little crow's feet at the corners of his eyes from where he stood. He lowered his voice. "By the way, I meant to tell you—that dog was all right. I went back and checked. No sign of anything."

She let out her breath. "Thanks for doing that."

"So, what's up?"

"This Secret Admirer thing has me completely stumped. I've studied the handwriting, I've listened around, I've asked questions, and I've watched to see if anyone looks at me a little more than they should. Everything comes up blank. Have you heard anything?"

"No, Shan, I haven't heard a thing. Sorry."

She glanced from side to side, to be sure they were alone in the office. "What about Gary? You heard what he said at the restaurant."

"You mean about the chocolate kiss? I think he heard that from Kathy."

Shannon's stomach clenched. She'd tried so hard to keep the Secret Admirer secret. She didn't know word was floating around the office. "You mean Kathy knows? Who else knows?"

"I don't think anyone knows anything specific. The same day you asked me if I'd heard anything, Kathy came into the dispatch office and asked Bryan if he had chocolate kisses. Kathy said Nanci had asked her for one because Faye asked Nanci, and she was wondering if someone had given them out and she'd missed one."

Shannon gritted her teeth. Faye knowing something was going on would be her downfall, but it was too late to do anything about it now. "I guess it's a relief then that I know the source of the information. I won't have to take Gary seriously."

Todd shrugged his shoulders. "I wouldn't. Besides, you know what he's like. He's broken a few hearts around here. Jody, for one. Gary eats women like you for breakfast. He's not your type anyway."

She folded her hands in front of her on the desk. "And how do you know what my type is?"

He grinned and winked. "I just know. He's not your type."

She tipped her head to study Todd. Over the years he'd seen every male she'd dated. She wouldn't have wanted Todd to pick what kind of man would be her type for her life's mate; yet, she could certainly trust his judgment on who wasn't. From the time she was old enough to date, whenever she started to get serious about a boyfriend, along came Todd, telling her at least one major character flaw, usually in a belittling manner and at the worst possible moment. The trouble was, even though it hurt, Todd was always right in his assessment.

This time, though, Todd hadn't put her in a state of emotional upheaval, telling her what a loser her current boyfriend was. She knew Gary was a charmer and not a Christian. Of course, he was likable and intelligent, but that didn't make him suitable, at least not for her. But she wasn't going to tell Todd that once again he was right.

She shrugged. "I'll be the judge of that. By the way, I was talking to Mom last night. Since she knows we see each other every day, she asked me how your mother was doing."

All traces of Todd's grin disappeared. "About the same," he mumbled. "I should get in there before the phones start going crazy."

Before she had a chance to say another word, Todd hustled into the dispatch office.

Shannon suddenly regretted bringing up a tender subject. She didn't know what the problem was between Todd and his mother; she only knew it had existed before she met him. When she'd asked Craig, Craig wouldn't tell her anything. At first it annoyed her, because they never kept any secrets from one another until Todd came along. But, when she became a teen, she realized she didn't have to be privy to all Craig's inner thoughts and knowledge, especially about his friends. Nor had she wanted to share all her thoughts with Craig anymore.

Just before she moved out, at the height of her frustration with Todd, she'd seen him come over for a visit. Because she didn't want Todd to drive her to the edge of insanity, she'd ducked into the kitchen, meaning to go out the back door instead of the front. Before she left, she'd overheard Craig ask Todd if his mother did "it" again. But all she heard in reply was muffled sobs.

She didn't know men did that. She'd heard women cry, but never a man. Until that day, she hadn't considered that Todd's problems at home could be so serious. She knew a social worker was involved with the family, but she'd always assumed it had something to do with social assistance, since he had no father and his mother never seemed to hold down a job.

Regardless of his mother's employment history, Shannon figured out then that Todd must have been living in a dysfunctional environment if one question about his mother could cause him to break down like that. From that day on, whenever Todd did something to hurt or embarrass her, she told herself he was acting like a wounded puppy, striking back at her for whatever was striking at him. It didn't make it any less painful for her, nor did it make it right, but it did provide an excuse.

That was also the day that despite how much he tormented her, Shannon had begun to pray for Todd, although not as regularly as she felt she should have.

Faye and Brenda's arrival in the office turned Shannon's thoughts to her upcoming payroll deadline. Right on schedule, Gary appeared with the drivers' time sheets.

"Hi, Shannon," he said, dropping them in her basket.

"Thanks, Gary," she muttered as she finished her current calculation.

He leaned forward. "Anything else I can do for you?"

Shannon slid a piece of paper across the desk and handed him her pencil. "Yes. Can you write something for me?"

He grinned and returned the pencil. "Sorry. I won't let you catch me. Nice try, though. Maybe we can go out for coffee or dinner one night and discuss what's going on."

In your dreams, she thought. "Maybe," she said.

"Great. It's a date then."

Before she could refute him, he turned around.

Shannon sighed as Gary walked away. She'd done a lot of thinking about every man she came in close contact with at work, Gary included. Not only was Gary intelligent, he had control issues, and he was also cagey. Being second only to the terminal manager, Gary had access to the building any time he pleased—days, nights, and weekends. Even if Gary wasn't the Secret Admirer, he had access to her desk when no one else was around, and he could easily have seen a note left for her, even if he didn't put it there. She could see him trying to lead her on, to get what he thought he could from another man's work. She'd seen him do such things professionally; she had no doubts he would do them personally.

But she wasn't positive he wasn't the Secret Admirer. If he was, she thought she might faint.

She doubted he was, though. The notes had an emotional flare she couldn't pin down. She was sure they sometimes didn't come out quite right because the Secret Admirer was working so hard at rhyming, but the message was clear. Someone had a crush on her, and he meant every word he said.

Gary wasn't the type to be poetic. He had a sharp wit and an analytical mind. If he turned to poetry, she was sure Gary's poetry would be more trendy and stylish, and he would certainly use more flare and alliteration in his choice of words.

Todd, on the other hand, might write like this, except she knew he wasn't capable of rhyming any words with more than a single syllable. The Secret Admirer used words she would never have dreamed of rhyming; yet they did.

Shannon looked toward the dispatch office.

She was sorry she'd put Todd in an awkward position, bringing up something that disturbed him when he should have been concentrating on his work. She knew he had some kind of difficulty with his mother, even as an adult. Craig told her Todd had started to change after he'd moved out and into his own place, just before Shannon moved out on her own. According to Craig, Todd became a Christian shortly after that. Now that she'd been working with him for a few months, she could see he was a changed man, not just because of his Christianity, but something else, too. She would never have thought Todd would mature, but he had.

But becoming a Christian didn't mean his struggles with his family would end. She'd known it was a sensitive subject, and she never should have asked him such a thing at work. For the first time, Shannon owed Todd an apology.

Until the opportunity arose to talk to him, Shannon resumed her work. Before she knew it, Faye was standing in front of her desk, and her stomach was starting to rumble.

"Faye, if you don't mind, I'm going to wait for half an hour and take my lunch break with Todd. There's something I have to talk to him about. Do you mind?"

Faye's eyes widened. "What did he do?"

Shannon smiled. "He didn't do anything. I just have to talk to him about something."

Faye's cheerful demeanor sagged. "Oh. Well, have fun."

Shannon couldn't help but feel sorry for Faye. She knew Faye had a crush on Todd, and it was a big one. But the more she thought about Todd—and Faye—the more she thought Faye needed someone more solid and grounded in their faith.

Like her brother Craig. . .

Shannon brightened. "I'm not going to have fun. It's something I have to talk to him about. I'll catch you at coffee time."

The next half hour was the slowest of her life, second only to the half hour she once spent trying to find a clear stream as a suitable habitat for a poor, displaced frog on death's doorstep.

As soon as Todd exited the dispatch room, Shannon hit *save* on her computer and followed him into the lunchroom.

He walked straight for the fridge and removed his lunch. When he turned around and saw her, his eyes widened. "What are you doing here?"

Shannon grinned, reached around him, and removed her own lunch. "I work here, and it's lunchtime. Mind if I share your table?"

His eyes widened even more. "Not at all."

Before they ate, they paused for a word of thanks. Shannon thought it special that for once, she wasn't the only one to pray out loud softly at work, as she always did with Faye.

Today Todd prayed. He wasn't eloquent, and his words didn't flow smoothly, but they came from his heart, and that was what counted.

While Shannon sprinkled dressing on her salad, she replayed his prayer in her mind. The more time she spent with Todd, the more she saw that Craig was right. Todd had changed, in many ways. She hadn't given him enough credit, and she felt guilty.

"I was wondering—have you ever been to any other church besides the one you attend now?"

Todd took a big bite of his sandwich. "Nope."

She started to nibble her carrot sticks. "You might enjoy going to a smaller service, one where there's more interaction and more opportunity to ask questions. I have an idea. Why don't you come to my church with me next Sunday? I think you'll like it."

"You're asking me to go to church with you?"

Suddenly, Shannon realized that was what she had done. "I guess I am."

His whole face brightened. "Sure. I think I'd like that. Is that why you wanted to have lunch with me?"

Shannon felt her cheeks heat up. "Not really. I think that was a spur-of-the-moment thing. Not that I'm going to change my mind. I wanted to apologize for this morning."

Todd started to cough and gulped down his mouthful, almost choking. "Apologize? To me? For what?"

"For bringing up a touchy subject here, where it had no place. That was poor timing on my part, and I apologize."

His cheeks reddened. "I appreciate it, but I think I'm the king of bad timing. Please don't think you ever owe me an apology for anything."

Shannon grinned at him. "Too late. I already apologized, and it's too late to take it back. By the way, I heard you did a great job in calming down one of the customers today."

"And I hear you cleared up a big muddle after Bryan messed up Jason's time sheet."

In contrast to the previous half hour, the lunch break flew by so fast Shannon didn't know where the time went.

She also had a feeling the week would be short, too. She didn't know if it was smart to invite Todd to her church, but she couldn't rescind her invitation. So she would make the best of it.

❧

Todd smiled as he worked. It still wasn't a date, but going to church with Shannon was the next best thing. Especially since she was the one who invited him.

He began entering a new pickup into the computer when he heard Shannon's name come up in Gary and Rick's conversation behind him.

Todd made a typo, backspaced, and kept typing, slowly, paying more attention to their words than to the pickup instructions. He didn't want to hear Gary telling Rick what he would like to do on a date with Shannon, but he couldn't stop listening. Something about his words gave Todd the impression it sounded less like a fantasy and more as if Gary thought it was a real possibility Shannon would participate.

In fact, the more he listened, the more it sounded as if Gary and Shannon had a date planned.

Todd's stomach churned. They'd just shared their lunch break, and Shannon hadn't told him she was going out on a date with Gary. If she had, he'd have told her a few of the things Gary said behind her back.

As Todd finished typing the entry, Gary appeared beside him.

"I thought you'd like to know Shannon's falling for it. One day soon, I'll have her."

Todd spun around to face Gary. "I don't think so. Shannon's not that way." He opened his mouth, wanting dearly to snap at Gary that Shannon had high moral standards, something Gary didn't, but self-preservation stopped him. He was still in his initial probation period, Gary was his boss, and Todd desperately needed the job. He scrambled to reword his statement, without pointing fingers. "You do know Shannon goes to church every Sunday?"

Gary's eyebrows rose; then he made a sly smirk. "You never know, but maybe one day I'll be going to church, too."

Gary spun on his toes, laughed heartily, walked into his office, and closed the door.

Todd's mind raced. From what he'd seen so far, Gary would never set foot in a church. But he'd also seen that Gary was wily. He didn't know what was so funny, but he had a feeling he had to find out. While he would have liked to see Gary open his heart to spiritual things, he wouldn't put it past him to attend church solely to impress Shannon. Gary had already used his position and authority to threaten him, without saying so directly. Todd feared he would also try to pressure Shannon in the same way, and he didn't want to see that happen. Gary's decisions carried a lot of weight. He worried Shannon might weaken if Gary turned on the charm; but he also feared what might happen if Shannon didn't do what the man wanted and he didn't take it well.

What made the situation worse was that Gary wouldn't have tried to get Shannon now if it hadn't been for his seeing Todd's Secret Admirer note. The whole thing was his fault.

Somehow, Todd had to find out what Gary was planning and warn Shannon.

He hoped she would listen and take him seriously. He'd told her so often why all her dates and boyfriends were wrong; he wasn't sure she would listen to him anymore.

Until he could find out a way to get Gary to confide in him so he could tell Shannon, he could only advise her to be careful. Then, on Sunday, he could take her out for lunch after church, and finally, they could have their first date. Maybe, if the time was right, he could tell her how he felt, and he wouldn't have to worry about Gary anymore.

Todd smiled. He could hardly wait until Sunday.

ten

"Hey, Shan. It's me. Todd. Let me in."

The buzzer sounded. Todd hurried to catch the elevator and was soon standing in front of Shannon's apartment door.

The door opened. Shannon stood in front of him wearing jeans and a T-shirt. A towel was wrapped around her hair. He smiled as he inhaled the heady aroma of her apple-scented shampoo, stronger than ever because her hair was still wet. As if he didn't think enough of Shannon, now every time he smelled apples, he'd think of her even more.

"I was getting ready to go out. What are you doing here?"

His smile disappeared. "Where are you going?"

Her brow creased. "It's Thursday night. I'm going to Bible study."

"Oh. Sorry."

"Do you go at your church? I know there are several groups to choose from."

"Yes. But I go Wednesday. Craig and I went last night." He had come because he didn't want to wait for Sunday and had wrongly assumed she also attended her home group on Wednesday night.

"Since you're here, do you want to come with me?"

Todd followed her as she returned to her room and started blow-drying her hair. "Sure. I'd like that. If I'm invited."

"Anyone is invited."

He didn't want to contemplate the impersonal nature of her invitation. He only wanted to talk to her in private.

But since he couldn't talk while she dried her hair, Todd sauntered into the living room and sat down on the couch.

Accompanying her tonight wasn't what he had planned, but it wasn't a bad thing. He would still be alone with her for part of the evening, and in that time, they could still talk. A few days ago, when they'd taken a late lunch break and were alone together, he'd had a very enjoyable time, and unless he was mistaken she had, too.

He could see the start of a beautiful relationship, and he wanted to start it today.

Shannon emerged from her room, her hair fluffy and bouncing with the natural wave he liked so much. "We have to leave in ten minutes. I hope you had something to eat before you got here."

"Yes, I did. You don't have to worry about feeding me. I just thought—"

The buzzer for the door cut off his words.

Shannon picked up the telephone. "Come on up," she said as she pushed the button.

"Who's that?"

"It's Craig. I have to talk to him about something, and he said he'd come with me. Now you're coming, too. This is going to be a regular party, isn't it?"

He tried to smile. "Yeah. A party."

Until they started working together, every time he'd been out with Shannon, it was because she'd tagged along with Craig. While he hadn't minded being a threesome before, today he wasn't in the mood to share her with her brother.

Shannon opened the door to let Craig in. Immediately, Craig turned to Todd.

"I thought I recognized your car in the visitor parking. Long time no see, huh?"

"Yeah," Todd muttered. "Since about this time yesterday."

"Look at this—the three of us together. Just like old times."

Todd didn't comment. He didn't want old times. He wanted

to make new times. Without Shannon's brother hanging over his head, watching him, protecting his little sister.

"Do you remember the last time the three of us were together?"

"Yeah. We were at church."

Craig shook his head. "That's different. I was thinking about that time just before Shan moved out. We were at the mall."

As best he could recall, the last time they were together in public they had been shopping and bumped into Shannon and her friends. It was so long ago he couldn't remember anything about the day, except that it had been good for their male egos to spend the afternoon with Shannon and five or six of her friends.

Shannon's eyes narrowed as she turned to stare at Todd. "I remember that. We all went into the coffee shop together for lunch."

Todd tried to remember why that detail would have been important.

Her eyes narrowed even more. "You went into the aisle, got down on one knee with a drink in your hand, and started singing Happy Birthday at the top of your lungs. That would have been bad enough, but it wasn't my birthday, and you knew it."

Suddenly, it all came back. Shannon had wanted a piece of chocolate cake, and she hadn't had enough money in her wallet to cover both lunch and dessert.

He pasted on a grin that he hoped wasn't as phony as it felt. "I was just trying to get you a free piece of cake."

"I can't remember the last time I'd been so embarrassed. But of course, the last time would also have had something to do with you."

All thoughts of how much progress he'd made in obtaining a wee bit of forgiveness evaporated.

Craig laughed out loud. "That was so funny! You should have seen your face!"

Todd smiled sheepishly. Back then, her face hadn't looked too cheery, nor did it now. In fact, Todd was glad they were going to a Bible study, where he hoped it would be stressed that God desired people to forgive those who hurt them.

Todd cleared his throat. "I think it's time to leave. Whose car are we taking?"

"Yours. I'm almost out of gas."

During their ride down the elevator, Todd wished Craig would run out of gas. Craig, in his wisdom, brought up another "amusing" trip down memory lane. Then he detoured on yet another memory in the car. Before Craig retold a fourth instance which involved Todd's humiliating poor Shannon, Todd managed to change the subject. However, he feared his efforts were too little, too late.

Throughout the lesson, Todd sat beside Shannon because he was the only one present who had not brought a Bible. He remained cautious in his comments and questions and tried to honor Shannon in his behavior.

When they returned to her apartment, Craig sat down on the couch, ready to talk about whatever it was Shannon had called him for in the first place. Todd took that as his cue to leave.

She walked Todd to the door.

"Before I go, I wanted to talk to you about something."

She glanced back at the opening to the living room, then back at him. "Go ahead, but remember Craig is waiting for me. I have to talk to him, and we all have to get up early for work tomorrow."

He stepped closer and picked up her hands, holding them gently while he spoke. "I just want you to be careful about Gary. Make sure you pray about it before you do anything. I really don't think he's your Secret Admirer. Be careful with him."

Her voice skipped. "Of course. . ."

"I'll see you tomorrow, and I can hardly wait until Sunday when I go to your church with you."

Before she could tell him she changed her mind, Todd turned and left.

❧

"Hi, Shannon."

Shannon laid her pencil down and folded her hands on the desk in front of her. "Hi, Gary. Is there something I can do for you?"

Gary crossed his arms, leaned on the edge of her desk, and grinned. "Yes. You can join me for dinner tonight."

Shannon studied Gary. Within the company, he was above her on the corporate ladder, second in command at their branch. While he didn't have any direct authority over her, she knew he was in a position of influence with the company. On the personal side, she knew Gary was young to be in his position, which was a good testimony to his management skills. While she didn't know his exact age, she guessed he was eight years older than she was.

Being a non-Christian, that also meant he had much more worldly experience than she did, both in the dating arena and in dealing with people in general. Gary's reputation preceded him, and his reputation told her this was a situation she didn't want to get involved with. Shannon tended to keep to herself and stayed within her church circles. She wasn't unhappy doing that. Instead, she felt safe and comfortable in her protected circle of friends and Christian family.

Secret Admirer or not, she made her decision.

"I don't know if going out for dinner with you is a good idea. We have to work together, regardless of what happens, if you know what I mean."

He leaned closer. "I know that, but I've been doing a lot of thinking lately. I know you go to church faithfully, and I was wondering if I could go with you on Sunday. But first I have a few questions."

Shannon's eyes widened. "You do?"

Gary nodded. "Yes. I thought you'd be the best person to ask."

Shannon often prayed she could be a good witness at her workplace, to be able to live in a way that people wouldn't write her off as a religious fanatic, yet still live her life to God's glory. She thanked God she could see the fruit of her efforts when someone like Gary could be interested in learning more about Jesus Christ as his Savior.

"I'd be happy to answer any questions you have, although here in the middle of the office isn't the best place."

"I know. That's why I thought we could go out for dinner."

Shannon checked the page on her calendar to be sure. "I actually have plans for tonight. Saturday, too. But I can still pick you up on Sunday morning."

Gary's smile dropped. "I don't know. . . ."

Shannon smiled. "Don't be shy. There's nothing to be afraid of. Give me your address, and I'll pick you up about a quarter to ten."

"I would prefer to pick you up."

Shannon forced herself to keep smiling. She thought it would be a good idea for her to be the one providing transportation, because if she were transporting him, it would be harder for Gary to change his mind at the last minute. But for now, she had to take any opportunity she could find to get Gary to church.

She scribbled her address on a piece of paper and slid it across the desk. "Okay. You can pick me up at a quarter to ten."

Gary grinned, winked, and tucked the note into his pocket. "See you then," he said as he returned to his office.

Shannon glanced to the dispatch area where Todd was. While it was good to bring a newcomer to church, this did present a complication. She had already arranged to pick up Todd for church on Sunday; but now she wouldn't have her car, and she'd also be with Gary. She thought Todd, a fairly new Christian, would understand. In fact, Shannon was certain Todd could relate to where Gary was now, since it wasn't that long ago Todd was searching for answers and found them.

She returned to her work. Tonight she planned to have dinner with Craig and some friends from her old church. She figured she'd see Todd there also, so she could talk to him tonight. She was sure Todd would be as happy as she was to know Gary would be at church on Sunday.

❧

"Pardon me? Did I hear you right?"

Shannon leaned closer to Todd so the rest of the people at the table wouldn't hear. "Yes, you heard me right. Isn't that exciting? He even said he has questions."

She backed up to gauge Todd's reaction, but instead of the smile she'd expected when she told him Gary would be coming to church with her, Todd's face turned to stone.

"I'll believe that when I see it."

All the joy seeped out of her. "I can't believe you aren't excited. The only thing is that he wants to take his own car, so I can't pick you up as we agreed. I hope that's okay."

Todd blinked, laid his fork down, and stared at her. "I can't believe you've suddenly turned gullible. He doesn't want to learn about God. He wants to learn about you."

"You don't know that."

Todd's eyes narrowed. "Yes, I do."

"Don't you think it's possible for him to listen if God is poking him and telling him to check out his options? Even murderers and people in jail can have a change of heart."

"I suppose."

"Then it's possible for Gary to want to discover God, too, don't you think?"

Shannon waited for Todd to say something. She didn't think she'd asked him a hard question. She'd prayed for Todd fairly often after overhearing about his mother, but she'd also prayed for him over the years because God told everyone to pray for their enemies. She wouldn't have thought it possible for him to open his hardened heart and become the man he was today, unless she'd witnessed the change herself. If it was possible for Todd, then it could happen with Gary.

Other people in their group chatted gaily, and the quiet murmur of voices echoed through the restaurant. But between her and Todd, the silence was so thick it shouted. When Todd was silent too long, Shannon crossed her arms and glared at him.

His voice dropped to a disgruntled whisper. "I guess," he muttered, barely loud enough for her to make out his words.

Before she could rebuke him for his bad attitude, Craig leaned forward from across the table. "What's going on?" He turned to Todd. "If you're doing something to upset my little sister, I'll have to take you outside."

Both of them stared at Craig.

"I'm not your little sister anymore, Craig."

He smiled. "Until we're both old and gray, you'll always be my little sister. All I know is that you two seem to be spending a lot of time together lately, and I don't mean just at work. If he's causing you trouble, I can take him outside and beat him up for you."

Shannon continued to stare at her brother. When she talked to Craig about her job and the possibility of his meeting Faye, Todd had come up in the conversation. She'd let it slip that she'd bumped into him at the bookstore, then again, mentioned being together when all her workmates went out for dinner. Plus Craig had seen Todd at her apartment yesterday.

Of course she didn't tell him about the time she hit the

dog with her car and Todd kissed her. She knew Craig was only kidding about beating up Todd. However, she had a feeling that if she told Craig he'd kissed her, it would come to blows between them, friends or not.

She narrowed her eyes, trying to look stern when really her insides were trembling. "I think I can handle Todd by myself."

"Are you sure?" He glanced back and forth between her and Todd, who remained silent. "It's just that in the past getting you two together in the same room was, well, not altogether pleasant." He leaned back in the chair and grinned. "Did Mom and Dad tell you? I'm thinking of trading in my car and getting a new one. Brand-new."

Shannon sat back and listened to Craig prattle on about the car he was looking at, along with a lengthy list of all its features. She noticed Todd still didn't say anything.

He truly was a mystery. Shannon had seen only his comic side, and most of that from the receiving end. Lately, she'd seen so much else. When she'd asked him about his mother, it was as if a brick wall had gone up around him. Now he sat in brooding silence. If she didn't know better, she would have thought he was angry that she was planning to spend time with Gary. But that was ridiculous. For Todd to be angry would indicate he was jealous, and that idea was so far fetched it didn't deserve any further consideration.

After everyone was finished and the group had broken up, she found herself leaving at the same time as still-brooding Todd. To her surprise, he followed her to her car and stood beside her while she fished her keys out of her purse.

Finally, Todd broke the strained silence. "I don't know why you won't listen to me. Gary isn't the least bit interested in learning about God. He's using this as a way to earn points. He's just picking something he feels is close to your heart and taking advantage of it. I hope you don't trust him, because if I were a woman, I sure wouldn't. He doesn't want to change. He just wants to have a little fun with you and nothing more."

Shannon's hand froze with the key inserted in the lock. She turned to face Todd. "Don't you think you're being rather harsh? And *very* judgmental."

"I'm being realistic."

"You haven't worked with him as long as I have, and you've been with him outside of work only once. How can you make that kind of accusation?"

"Stuff I've heard."

She crossed her arms. She knew Gary's reputation with the ladies, but that wasn't the issue. They had mentioned that regardless of what happened between them they would have to work together every day. She didn't agree to date Gary. In fact, she'd told him the opposite. She'd told him she was busy, but she still was happy to take him to church and answer any questions he had. "I wish you wouldn't be so quick to think the worst of Gary. I know he has his faults, but he's dedicated and intelligent. You should give him some credit."

"Credit for what? His good looks? The good job? Money? His fancy car?"

Shannon turned around and yanked the door open. "That's enough. I don't have to listen to you and your bad attitude."

"The only reason he's talking about going to church is that you have a reputation for not going out with anyone, even once, who doesn't go to church. That's it."

She slid inside the car. "I don't believe you."

She tried to close the door, but Todd grabbed it, preventing her from moving it. "It's the truth. I don't want him to take advantage of you. He's only looking for a good time."

Her blood boiled. "I know what I'm doing, Todd," she said harshly. She sucked in a deep breath and pulled the door, forcing him to release it or catch his fingers as it slammed.

She turned the key in the ignition, rolled down the window, and leaned her head out for one last parting comment as she drove away.

"Besides, for your information, he just might be my Secret Admirer."

eleven

Todd stood in front of the mirror and straightened his tie. His hand froze on the knot as he gave it a final tug. He closed his eyes.

He'd had a fight with Shannon. That was Friday night. He hadn't spoken to her since.

He'd let the sun go down on his anger. He'd also let Saturday's sun, a second night, go down on his anger.

He didn't know if he'd ever been so angry or so disappointed in himself.

Shannon hadn't listened to a thing he said; yet he'd been speaking the truth. Still, he had no right to be so angry. He'd had all night Friday, all of Saturday, and the early part of Sunday morning to think, giving him plenty of opportunity to sort things out.

Of course, Shannon would give Gary the benefit of the doubt if he said he was interested in learning about God. Her gentle and forgiving spirit was a big part of what made Shannon who she was. She was starting to open up at least to be friends. She'd put aside all the bad things he'd done to her and forgiven him. If she did that for Todd, she would do the same for Gary, who had never personally done anything to hurt or embarrass her, as Todd had.

In many ways, Gary deserved more of a chance than Todd did. And she was giving Gary the chance, too.

Todd was jealous, and he knew it. And that was another thing that hurt.

He knew what the man was like. Shannon had worked with Gary for longer than he had. Years. She knew Gary far

116

better than he did, which made it even worse that she would consider spending personal time with him. The thought of her hanging around with him and liking him was too much for Todd to bear.

What if she liked Gary more than she liked him. . . .

Todd opened his eyes and studied his reflection in the mirror. He'd just showered and shaved, and he'd gelled his hair meticulously into place. He'd bought some new toothpaste; his teeth hadn't been so white since his last trip to the dentist. His shirt and pants were clean and pressed. His tie was a perfect match, the most expensive one he owned, and it didn't even have a sound chip or flashing lights. He didn't get any better than this.

But this time, he needed more. If he wanted to look better than Gary, there was no competition. Gary was taller than he was and had one of those handsome faces that turned women's heads. He was in better physical condition because he worked out at the gym three times a week, since he had the money for it. If Todd were honest with himself, Gary was probably smarter than he was, too. When Todd became uncomfortable, he made jokes and displayed ridiculous behavior—anything to get a laugh to ease a difficult moment. Gary, on the other hand, oozed confidence and poise in everything he said and did.

On the surface, Gary had everything going for him. But beneath the trendy clothes and perfect hair and movie-star handsome face, Gary was pond scum. And Shannon was right. Todd knew he was being judgmental, but that didn't make him wrong. While everyone knew beauty was only skin deep, Shannon had to get past Gary's skin layer to see the real man. In doing so, he hoped Gary didn't do something to hurt her, either physically or emotionally.

After Gary's comment the other day, Todd should have figured out he would try to motivate Shannon to see him outside of work. Shannon was right; he was intelligent. The only reason she would see him would be to minister to him, so that was what Gary zeroed in on.

Despite what Todd thought was the reality of the situation, there was still a one-tenth-of-one-percent chance Gary might be sincere in his quest to know God. If that were so, then Todd was being worse than judgmental. He was being unfair. God had touched him when he had no thoughts of Him. Craig had tried to show him God's love ever since they'd been in their teens and often told Todd he'd been praying for him. Every time, Todd had scoffed and told him not to bother. Looking back, he had a feeling Shannon might have been praying for him, too.

If the two of them had been praying for him for ten years before he allowed God to touch him, then it happened, the same could happen with Gary. Todd was a sinner, just as Gary, and God loved Gary, too.

Todd looked around. He figured Shannon would be ten minutes early for the church service, as she was at work, regardless of whether she was driving or if Gary was picking her up.

Todd said a short prayer for wisdom and made his way to Shannon's church, not caring if she wanted him there or not.

He recognized Gary's car in the parking lot and parked nearby.

Once inside the building, he found them easily. Of course, Gary was dressed perfectly, in clothes Todd could never afford. Shannon wore a pretty skirt and blouse, with shoes the same color as the skirt. Over her top, she wore a sweater Todd knew her mother had knitted for her. Todd smiled. She wasn't fancy. She was just Shannon.

He wiggled the knot on his tie and approached them.

"Hey, Shannon, Gary. Good morning."

Shannon spun around in the blink of an eye. Gary turned more slowly.

"Todd!" Shannon gasped. "What are you doing here?"

He raised his hand and pressed his Bible to his chest. "It's Sunday. I came to church—which is where I go every Sunday morning. Your invitation to join you this morning still stands, doesn't it?"

Her face turned ten shades of red. "Of course," she muttered. "I just didn't expect you to come by yourself."

Todd smiled at her. "I'm not alone. I'm with friends now." He turned to Gary. "It's good to see you here in God's house." He forced himself to keep smiling, trying to tell himself he really meant his words. "Shall we find a seat?"

The three of them walked toward the sanctuary together. When they came to the entranceway, Gary stepped in front of Todd, forcing him to enter behind Gary. Before he could catch up to Shannon, Gary guided her into the nearest pew. He slipped in beside her, leaving enough room for Todd at the end.

Todd narrowed his eyes. He didn't want to sit beside Gary; he wanted to sit beside Shannon, and Gary knew it.

Once again, he forced himself to smile and stepped toward Gary. "Excuse me," he said. Not giving Gary a choice, he stepped in front of him, forcing him to tuck his legs to the side so Todd could get by. He then stepped gently past Shannon, as she also tucked her legs to the side, then sat beside her. Once seated, he turned to address them both at the same time. "I like to leave the aisle seat open. For elderly ladies."

Shannon smiled tenderly and rested her fingers on his forearm. "Oh, Todd, that's so sweet." She sighed.

Gary's ever-present friendly expression faltered for just a second. "That's a good idea. I'll have to remember that for next time."

Todd hoped there wouldn't be a next time, then mentally kicked himself, in case this was the one-tenth-of-one-percent chance that Gary was here for good and honest reasons that had to do with God and not specifically with Shannon.

When the service started, Todd noted the routine was similar to his own church's but not identical. Shannon's church was much smaller and geared more to a younger congregation than his own, which was the only church he'd ever attended. With the difference in mind, he was relieved to know all the songs except one. Even though singing wasn't one of his greatest strengths, he worshipped from his heart, trying not to notice Gary caught on quickly to the songs and sang better than he did.

Shannon's pastor preached a good message with a little more fire and brimstone than he was used to, about the parable of the man sowing his seed. Once Todd became accustomed to the pastor's animated speech and the shout of the occasional "Amen" from various members of the congregation, the enthusiasm of the pastor and the congregation became infectious. Todd almost called out an "Amen" to a point that hit home with him but held himself back because he didn't want to startle Shannon. Sitting between him and Gary, she didn't appear completely comfortable, and he couldn't blame her. He didn't want to make it worse for her.

Throughout the entire service, in between being enthralled with the pastor's words and writing notes on the back of the bulletin, Todd snuck a few sideways glances over Shannon at Gary. In a way, Todd hoped the pastor would have been more calm and sedate, allowing Gary to fall asleep. Instead he'd caught Gary sneaking sideways glances at him, probably hoping the same thing.

At the close of the service, Todd forced all thoughts of Gary out of his head and followed in his heart with the pastor's prayer and benediction. When most of the congregation called out an "Amen," he did, too, which caused Shannon to jump and Gary to stare at him, but he didn't care. The service had been great, with the possible exception of Gary being there.

As they filed toward the sanctuary's exit, he tried to push away the guilt he felt about being annoyed by Gary's presence. If the man truly was searching, the sermon had been great for him. If not, it wasn't Todd's place to judge, as Shannon had reminded him.

Todd gritted his teeth as Gary deliberately stepped in front of him at the doorway between the sanctuary and the foyer, nearly landing on his foot. He decided his guilt was again misplaced. From the way Gary kept trying to put distance between Todd and Shannon and the fact he was becoming more aggressive about it, the one-tenth-of-one-percent chance Gary was there for legitimate reasons was becoming exponentially smaller.

Back in the foyer, Shannon introduced both Todd and Gary to other members of the congregation. After a bit of small talk and people welcoming them to the church, Gary suggested he and Shannon go for lunch.

Todd chose to ignore that Gary's invitation had been worded not to include him. He grinned enthusiastically so Gary would look like a shmuck in front of Shannon if he said anything about Todd's not being invited. "That sounds great." He turned to Shannon. "I think you were saying that most of your congregation goes to that pancake place across from the skating rink. But I also remember your saying parking was pretty tight. Maybe I should go with you guys, then you can just drop me off back here when we're finished so I can pick up my car."

Gary's eyes narrowed. In response, Todd widened his smile.

Shannon tapped one finger to her chin. "You know, that's a pretty good idea. Some people park their cars in the rink's lot; but there are signs warning people that if they're not there to skate, they could get towed."

Todd nodded. "I think I've had enough problems with my car lately. I'll leave it here. Let's go."

Gary didn't say much as they walked out to the parking lot. Once at the car, Todd slid into the back, which he didn't mind. He knew Gary wasn't going to make any efforts to include him in the conversation, but this way he could keep an eye on what was happening in the front, with Gary very aware he was being watched.

While they waited for a table, Todd could tell Gary was pushing himself to make polite conversation with him there. After they were seated and their orders taken, Todd decided it was time to show Shannon the level of Gary's sincerity about learning about God.

He tried to ignore that Gary was sitting beside Shannon in the booth and he wasn't. But this way gave him a better opportunity to watch what Gary was doing. Todd could see him eye-to-eye instead of peeking up from between the bucket seats as he had in the car.

With his elbows on the table, Todd cradled his coffee cup in both hands and made deliberate eye contact with Gary over the top of the steaming coffee.

"Shannon tells me this is the first time you've been to church. What did you think of the service?"

"It was interesting," Gary replied, smiling politely.

Todd nodded. "Yes. He really made me think. I thought it was an interesting question, asking what kind of ground we were, as an individual."

"Yes. He allowed for a lot of introspection."

Todd stared right into Gary's eyes. "Do you remember the four types of ground?"

"Not really. Although I saw you writing notes, so you have more likelihood of remembering."

"That may be true, but that's not what I was writing down. The four different types of ground are"—Todd set the cup back into the saucer and counted off on his fingers as he spoke—"on the path, in the rocks, among the thorns, and on good soil."

Gary's expression glazed over for a few seconds, indicating to Todd that Gary hadn't been paying attention and didn't want to be paying attention now. "Yes, that's right," he said.

The more Todd thought about it, and watching Gary's face now, Todd suddenly understood why Gary hadn't paid attention. According to the parable, the ground accepted the seed initially, and all but one type fell away for various reasons. Gary's situation didn't apply to this because he had no desire to sample the seed in the first place. He only wanted to sample Shannon.

Todd picked up his cup again, suddenly needing something to do with his hands, rather than reaching across the table and wringing Gary's neck.

He smiled nicely, hoping his face wouldn't crack. He opened his mouth, about to comment on the possibility of giving Gary a Bible, when Shannon clinked her cup down into her saucer.

"I think that's enough talk about the sermon. This isn't a question-and-answer period." She glared at him from across the table. "Todd," she said firmly. She turned her head slightly toward Gary. "Did you see the construction at the mall on the way here? It looks as if they're expanding the building. I wonder where everyone is going to park."

They spent the remainder of lunch making small talk about nothing in particular. Gary insisted on paying for all three lunches, which griped Todd but looked good to Shannon.

To Todd's surprise, Gary dropped off Shannon first, instead of returning to the church parking lot so Todd could get his car. Because Todd didn't want it to look as if he was following them, which he was, he stayed in the car while Gary walked Shannon to the door. Part of him was glad he was taking

Shannon home first. This way, good manners dictated that Shannon not invite Gary in and that Gary didn't take too long saying good-bye, since Todd was waiting in the car.

But this also meant he would be alone with Gary traveling from Shannon's apartment to the church parking lot.

The thought made Todd break out into a cold sweat.

He looked at the empty front seats, thinking he should have the grace to move from the back seat into the front. But the last thing he wanted to do was sit beside Gary because that meant he would have to talk to him.

By the time Gary returned, Todd was settled in the front seat, buckled in, ready to go, and praying they caught every light green.

The second Gary started the engine, Todd leaned forward and turned the radio up, not caring what kind of station it was or what was playing.

Even though the music was loud, the lack of conversation hung in the air between them like a cold, looming black cloud. When they were a block from the church, Gary reached forward and turned the radio down. The lightness of Gary's tone was completely negated by his words. "You know, Sanders—I don't know if you think you're trying to be funny, but you might notice I'm not laughing."

Steeling his courage, Todd turned to Gary. "You know, for once, I wasn't trying to be funny."

Gary kept his face forward, not looking at Todd as he spoke, which only seemed to accent his words. "I think it would be in your best interests if you kept out of this and started minding your own business. What I do with Shannon is none of your concern. I like the way you do your job, and I enjoy working with you, but I would hate to suddenly start finding too many mistakes while you're still on probation."

Todd's head spun. He had expected Gary to confront him, but he hadn't expected this.

Before he could put two thoughts together to respond, the car stopped in the parking lot beside his car, the only one in the entire lot.

Gary still didn't turn his head but kept his face forward, watching ahead of him through the windshield. "I'll see you tomorrow at work, Sanders. Good day."

Todd exited Gary's car quickly.

He stabbed the key into the lock, slid in, and slammed the door. Instead of starting the car, he whacked the steering wheel with his fist and muttered under his breath.

He was only trying to protect Shannon—from Gary and from herself. He hadn't considered that his actions could mean losing his job. He needed the job. If he lost it, he wouldn't be the only one to suffer, and he couldn't let that happen.

And if Gary would stoop so low as to threaten Todd, then he wondered if the man would use his power and authority at work on Shannon. While Gary wasn't her supervisor, as he was Todd's, he was still second in command over the branch. As such, he had some degree of authority over every department, even if only by influencing the one person higher than Gary in the corporate ladder.

Todd clenched his teeth as he started the car. Shannon didn't know who she was getting herself involved with. He doubted she had the slightest idea of what the man who said he wanted to learn about God really wanted. Or what he was willing to do to get it.

But Todd intended to tell her.

It took every ounce of Todd's self-control to drive within the posted speed limit to Shannon's apartment.

The time it took for him to park the car, walk to the main door, press the button, and wait for her to respond gave Todd time to calm down and think more clearly.

He was angry with Gary, but he couldn't be angry with Shannon. She was only doing what she thought was best. He couldn't belie her efforts in what she saw as the right and noble thing, even though she was wrong.

Shannon's voice crackled through the intercom. "Hello?"

He cleared his throat and tried to sound cheerful. "Hi, Shan. It's me. Todd. Want to do dinner?"

"Todd?" For a few seconds, he heard static sparking through the metal grating. "Uh—it's kind of early for dinner; we just had lunch. But come up. I guess."

When the elevator door swooshed open on Shannon's floor, he found her waiting in the hallway outside her door. She stood with her arms crossed, and she wasn't smiling. "What are you really doing here? Even you can't be thinking about eating again."

"I wanted to talk to you about something." He glanced both ways down the hall. He was prone to public displays and appreciated when he had an audience that was amused by his antics, but that was when nothing important was at stake. This time he wanted everything he said kept between him and Shannon and not her neighbors. "Can we go inside?"

Shannon stepped back and extended one arm but said nothing.

The second the door closed, Todd could no longer hold back. "I don't think you have any idea what you're dealing with. I came here to tell you to be very careful with Gary. You're in way over your head."

Her eyes narrowed. "I thought I knew what he was like, but I'm wondering if I've been wrong. On the way to church, he talked to me about how he has to put on a tough, hard-edged facade in front of the men at work to earn and keep their respect. He says part of that includes acting like a ladies' man."

Todd crossed his arms. "He's only telling you what you want to hear."

Her voice lowered. "I'm not stupid, Todd. I've seen him in action at work. I'm only saying we talked, and I think I have to make some allowances for him. I at least have to think about it."

"You don't need to think about it. I wanted to give him the benefit of the doubt, too. He said something in the car, though, that made me realize not only have I been right, but he's even worse. And you can forget any romantic notions he has for you. He's only trying to mislead you. He has nothing good or noble in mind for you. You shouldn't be seeing him outside work. And that includes church. You think you're safe on Sunday morning, but you're not. Not with him."

"What did he tell you in the car?"

"I'd rather not say now."

Shannon tipped her head and studied him, not saying anything while the seconds dragged on like hours. "Why are you doing this? What do you have against Gary?"

"I have nothing against him."

Her posture stiffened even more. "It sure sounds like it to me. And besides his interest in learning more about God and Jesus Christ, he said he wanted to be sure I liked chocolate kisses. It looks as if he might be my Secret Admirer after all. He's hinting, trying to build the suspense. He's waiting for the right moment to tell me."

Todd's restraint exploded in a puff of smoke. He waved one hand in the air, barely able to keep from yelling. "Can't you see he's lying to you? He's just using that because he knows it's a soft spot with you. Just like going to church is a soft spot with you."

"How dare you!"

He stepped closer and lowered his voice. "Shannon, I'm not saying these things to make you angry. I'm only saying this out of concern because I, uh"—he swallowed hard and cleared his throat—"I like you a lot. I don't want to see you get hurt, and I think your spending time with Gary is a bad idea. I only want to help you."

"I have to finish what I started, with or without you. Surely you agree that Gary needs someone to walk through this with him. Maybe next week you should go to your own church."

Todd's heart sank. "What?"

She checked her watch. "And I can't go out to dinner with you. I had already made plans to go out with a friend for dinner. In fact, I think you should leave now."

Todd felt as if he'd been smacked in the chest with a two-by-four. He wanted so much to reveal his proof that Gary was lying to her, but he couldn't tell her he was her Secret Admirer now. He'd had dreams of the right moment—in a romantic atmosphere, wrapped in each other's arms, soft music playing in the background. Maybe even feeding her chocolate kisses by hand or sharing chocolate kisses between real ones. Not only was there nothing romantic about this moment, but she was throwing him out of her home. She was so angry with him that he had a feeling she'd never believe him.

"Fine," he muttered, trying to take her rejection like a man. "I guess I'll see you at work tomorrow." He turned on his heel and stomped to the door.

As he stepped into the hallway, he felt Shannon's fingers touch his arm, stopping him in his tracks.

"Todd, wait. I want you to understand why I'm doing this. I have to give him a chance. God gives us all a chance, regardless of whether we deserve it or not. I have to do the same."

Todd's head spun. His thoughts and emotions had ricocheted in his head and heart in so many directions and on so many levels that he didn't know what to think anymore. He felt himself going into auto-pilot mode with his reaction.

He turned around. "So in other words you're telling me don't go away mad; just go away."

She smiled. He felt himself melting into a puddle on the floor.

"Yes, something like that. Good-bye, Todd."

The door closed.

Todd's brain was so numb he didn't remember the drive home, only that he was there.

He sat at the kitchen table and did the same thing he did every day when he couldn't get Shannon out of his mind. He tore a piece of paper out of the pad, opened the rhyming dictionary, and began to compose his newest poem.

Dearest Shannon,
  Your merciful spirit soothes my tortured soul

Todd grimaced and crumpled up the paper. He didn't want to acknowledge her anger or her forgiveness or that he was feeling rotten from arguing with her. Shannon was intelligent and perceptive. If he mentioned anything even remotely related to what had just happened, she might figure out why her Secret Admirer would say such things, then know who he was. He couldn't afford for that to happen. Not now. Not until everything was perfect between them.

He tore off a sheet of fresh paper and tried again.

Dearest Shannon,
  Your shining smile fills me with happiness

Todd flipped through the book and harumphed when he discovered there was no exact rhyme for happiness. He wadded up the paper and closed his eyes to picture Shannon in his mind before he started again.

Dearest Shannon,
  Like the sweet, clean scent of a tangy apple

Todd buried his face in his hands. That apple shampoo

was affecting him more than he thought. This time he ripped the paper into multiple pieces and pushed them to the center of the table.

> Dearest Shannon,
>   Like the sparkling spring sunshine in the month of May,
>   Like the sweet, clean scent of a fresh bouquet,
>   Like the beauty and fullness of a rose when it's blooming,
>   My love for you is all consuming.
>
>   Your Secret Admirer

Todd smiled. This was one of his best. In fact, it was so good he thought when the day came to reveal himself to Shannon, he would share a case of chocolate kisses and go to the florist and pick out a nice red rose. Or maybe one of those two-toned ones, because he knew she liked them.

As Todd tied the ribbon and attached the kiss, his thoughts drifted back to the situation with Gary. Of course, Shannon was right. God had given Todd more chances than he could count, when he was nowhere near looking for God's heart. He had to step back and let Shannon handle Gary in whatever way she thought best. Even though it hurt, Todd knew he would have to pray for Gary, even if it took ten years or more, just as Craig and Shannon had prayed for him.

The events of the day also proved to him he never wanted to fight with Shannon over Gary again. He didn't want to fight with her about anything. It was too painful. He'd put her through enough over the years without adding more tension. When he thought of what could have happened by fighting over Gary, he felt sick. He didn't want to lose her over something that needed to be in the Lord's hands.

Todd shut his eyes. His heart pounded. During the time Shannon spent with Gary, he couldn't help but worry that she might like Gary better than she liked him. Regardless of what Todd knew or heard, he had to leave that in the Lord's hands, too. The battle of love wasn't always won by the person who was the most deserving. Not that he deserved Shannon. He was trying his best to make things right from the past, though. He could only hope and pray it was enough.

He opened his eyes and stared blankly at the wall. If Shannon did choose Gary over him and Todd came out the loser, then it would be inappropriate for him, as the Secret Admirer, to keep telling her how much he loved her, because her heart would belong to another.

But that didn't mean he wouldn't keep an eye on her, just to be sure she was safe and happy.

twelve

"Hey, Shan. Are you going out for lunch with Gary again today?"

Shannon cringed at Nanci's question. In the last couple of weeks, she'd gone out with Gary almost every other day. She hadn't realized it had become a topic of conversation among the other staff, although she hadn't been trying to keep it a secret. Before she could tell Nanci she wasn't going out today, Faye piped up.

"No, she went out with Gary for lunch yesterday. She'll be staying here today because it's Todd's turn."

Nanci drew in her breath sharply. "Wow. I wish I had your love life."

Shannon steeled her nerve and turned toward Nanci. "It's not like that at all. Todd and I are just friends. The same with Gary."

She could tell from Nanci's expression and the expressions of those around who were listening that no one believed her.

"It's true," she muttered, as she resumed her work.

Unfortunately, her words were truer than she wanted them to be. She didn't have a love life. Gary was a ministry. Nothing more, nothing less. She wanted to keep things as they were now, which was the occasional lunch on a weekday and church on Sunday.

Shannon's hands paused over the keyboard.

Church on Sunday.

Without Todd.

She couldn't believe how much she missed him. Not that she really saw him any less—she saw him every day at work, plus she saw him for various reasons several times a week after working

132

hours and on weekends. But she missed not being with him during the Sunday worship services. She'd been with him two Sunday mornings, first at her old church, then at her new one; yet now she felt the loss when the seat on the other side of her was empty, which had been the last two Sundays.

Shannon sighed. She deeply regretted telling him not to come with her. After two weeks of being with him during the service, and now two weeks of not having him there, she had to admit she missed him. She wanted to take back her words but didn't know how.

Shannon glanced at the doorway leading to the dispatch office, where Todd was hard at work. He was still the same old Todd she'd always known, but at the same time, he was completely different. It didn't make sense, but it was true.

The day of their big argument about Gary, Todd had let it slip that he liked her. She could tell from his face he hadn't meant to say it out loud, which only emphasized he meant it.

She couldn't help herself. After all this time, she liked him, too. She didn't know when it happened, or why, but she found herself thinking about him often. If the man in question hadn't been Todd Sanders, she would have wondered if this was what it was like to fall in love.

Shannon closed her eyes. The pressures of her job were becoming too much for her. Surely, she was going insane.

She glanced to the side, at Faye, hard at work.

The meeting she'd set up between Faye and Craig had gone well. Craig, being Craig, had convinced Faye to attend a church service again. In fact, she'd heard about her first visit back to church in over three years from Todd, who sat with them that morning. He'd been relieved Faye was over the crush she had on him and encouraged she had responded well to the pastor's sermon.

She turned her head toward the doorway to the dispatch office.

She didn't want Todd to sit with Faye and Craig at her old church. She wanted Todd to sit with her and Gary at her new church.

She looked back at her computer screen, which had gone blank from inactivity.

It was true she had gone out to lunch a number of times in the last couple of weeks with Gary. She'd enjoyed the time she spent with him. But Gary mentioned repeatedly he felt rushed while they talked, and he didn't like it. Shannon felt the same way, as she had many things she wanted to say to him that couldn't be limited to five or ten minutes.

She wasn't sure when it started, but Gary began to ask, over and over, if they could go out in the evenings to talk. But the places he suggested weren't what Shannon considered conducive to talking about opening one's life to God. They were romantic getaways, places more expensive than she'd ever been. Even though Gary hadn't said so out loud, Shannon suspected that if she agreed, just by the atmosphere and what went with it, more would be expected of the relationship than ministry.

Lately, Gary had also been inquiring about a boyfriend. When she finally gave in and told him she had no boyfriend, his questions started becoming more personal, even suggestive.

She didn't want to cross that line or have that kind of relationship. At least, not with Gary.

Nanci's words about her "love life" replayed in her mind. Despite what Gary was hinting at, he was a ministry. For all the time she spent with Todd, he was an old friend, now that she could call him a friend. The only love she had in her life was her Secret Admirer, a man she didn't know. Or if she did know him, she didn't know who he was. So he didn't count.

Yet both Gary and Todd worked with her. In the months since she started receiving the notes, no other man in the office acted differently around her. Most of them barely noticed her at all; they only looked in her direction long enough to make sure their time cards landed in the right basket when they tossed them on her desk. Since she had no other candidates, either Gary or Todd could likely be the Secret Admirer.

Gary was a charmer. He knew what women liked, and women knew he knew. She could imagine Gary doing something romantic and fanciful to win the heart of a lady, especially because he was so aware that women soaked up his attentions. If pressed, Shannon had to admit she was not immune to Gary's charm, either. His polished manners and the way he presented himself suited the role of a handsome and dashing suitor.

The other possibility was Todd. Todd was—

Shannon shook her head. Todd was *not* the Secret Admirer.

She resumed her work until Faye told her it was time for lunch break. Faye ended up sitting with someone else, so she found herself once again sitting with Todd, as Faye had predicted.

As usual, Todd was in a happy mood, and soon, he had her laughing so hard she nearly choked on her salad.

Now was not the time to talk about Gary, about whom they had agreed to disagree. Before she could gather up her courage to ask Todd to join her and Gary the following Sunday morning, another employee appeared at their table to engage Todd in a conversation; one of the drivers had damaged a van.

While they talked, Shannon studied Todd. She would never have thought of him as responsible; yet he was a good fit in his position. He admitted the driver's degree of fault, but he also pronounced a fair judgment and recommended against disciplinary action for a number of good and valid reasons. Shannon knew Todd would stick up for her in the same way if something happened. Because Craig knew she had been seeing a lot of Todd, her brother continued to give her updates on his progress with the Lord. Yet, for all the changes, he was still the same old Todd.

When they were finally alone again, Todd turned to her and sighed. "I have to ask you something. I'm having my mom over for dinner tomorrow. Do you know what I can cook her that's good and healthy, too? Something with lots of vegetables. Remember it has to be easy, because I'm not very good in the kitchen."

Shannon smiled. Yes, he was still the same old Todd Sanders. She remembered one day when Todd and Craig had set something on fire in her mother's kitchen. Since it hadn't been an oil-based fire, Todd had used the sprayer from beside the kitchen sink to extinguish the fire. Her parents had arrived before the smoke residue cleared completely, but fortunately, the rest of the mess was cleaned up, except for one slightly blackened area on the hood above the stove, which remained to this day.

"I can't think of anything healthier than some nice stir-fried vegetables, maybe with cubed chicken and noodles. You can do that, can't you?"

Todd's eyebrows raised. "I don't know how to stir-fry noodles. I also don't know how to cook vegetables unless they come out of a can."

Shannon rolled her eyes. "Canned vegetables are already cooked."

"Really? Then I'm halfway there. Can I buy cooked noodles, too, and just mix them together?"

Shannon tipped her head to one side slightly. He looked on the verge of desperate. She didn't know why cooking vegetables for his mother was so important, instead of just cooking her a nice meal, but she didn't need to know. Something inside her wanted to help him. "I'm not doing anything tonight. If you want, we can go shopping together. I'll show you what to buy, and I can tell you how to cook it."

"I have a better idea. How about if I buy double of everything

I need, you show me how to cook it, and then I'll cook the second batch tomorrow by myself?"

She wanted to protest and tell him he wouldn't enjoy the same thing two days in a row. But she often stir-fried a meal one day, then enjoyed the leftovers more the next day when they were already cooked and all she had to do was reheat them.

More important, she needed a chance to be alone with Todd. It had been on her conscience for two weeks that she should apologize to him for the way she told him not to attend church with her when she took Gary. Also, she wanted to reinvite him and hope he accepted. She didn't know what was wrong between Todd and Gary, but ever since they'd attended church together Shannon detected a strain between them. Not only did Gary tend to be more critical of Todd, Todd stopped joking when Gary entered the room. She didn't want something she'd said or done to affect their working relationship, especially since Gary was Todd's supervisor. But first, she had to find out what was wrong so she could deal with it.

"That sounds like a great idea. It's time to get back to work. I'll see you at 4:30."

❧

An afternoon never passed so slowly.

Every minute felt like an hour.

At 4:30 sharp, Shannon walked into the dispatch office, her purse slung over her shoulder. "Ready to go?"

Todd looked up at the clock. "Actually, no. I have to wait for Dave to call in and let me know he doesn't need a helper. If he doesn't, then I can go."

"No problem. I'll be at my desk. I can always find something to keep me busy."

At 4:37, the radio beeped, signaling Dave's call. After Dave confirmed he didn't need a second man sent out, Todd packed up his paperwork and poked his head in Gary's office. Gary was busy typing on his computer, but he acknowledged Todd with a nod.

"I'm gone for the day," Todd said from the doorway, not stepping inside Gary's office.

"I hear you're doing something with Shannon."

Todd stiffened from head to foot. What he did on his own time was none of Gary's business. What he did with Shannon was especially none of Gary's business. But he wasn't going to hide the fact he spent time with her. Every day she didn't go out to lunch with Gary, Todd made sure he took his break at the same time as Shannon. Everyone saw them together, including Gary, and Todd didn't care. As far as everyone was concerned, they were old, childhood friends, and that was exactly what he wanted them to think. "That's right."

"She tells me she's not currently dating anyone. I trust that includes you, too."

Unfortunately, it did include him. In the time he'd spent with Shannon since he started leaving her the notes, the right moment had never come up to tell her how he felt. He rationalized the delay not by admitting his fear of rejection, but by telling himself she was still enjoying reading the notes every morning.

Todd crossed his arms and stretched himself to stand as tall as he could. "For now."

Gary continued to type on his computer. "Just making sure my options are open." Gary's hands stilled, and he raised his eyes to stare at Todd intently as he spoke. "And that they stay open."

"That's up to Shannon now, isn't it, Gary?" Before Gary could respond and before Todd said something he would regret later, he clamped his mouth shut. He spun around to leave and froze.

Shannon was standing in the doorway leading into the dispatch office.

Todd's heart pounded. She was standing where Gary couldn't see her. Since she hadn't spoken, he didn't know she was there. And Todd intended to keep it that way.

In two steps, he was at her side. Without speaking, he gently gripped her elbow, guided her so she turned around, and nudged her to start walking. She didn't say a word until they were outside in the parking lot.

"What was that all about? What's up to me?"

"Whether or not you decide to go out with him."

"Go out with him?" Shannon sputtered. "Why are you discussing with Gary who I'm going out with?"

Todd rammed one hand in his pocket for his keys. As he did so, his fingers brushed the note he'd intended to leave in Shannon's drawer but hadn't because they'd exited the building together. "I wasn't discussing anything. Gary brought it up, not me. I told him what you did is up to you. But I think you know by now how I feel about your seeing Gary."

Her face tightened. "And you know by now how I feel about him. This is my decision, as you said."

Todd's stomach clenched. He'd watched Gary pour his seductive routine over Shannon for the past couple of weeks. From what he'd seen, she was falling for it because she wasn't telling Gary to take a hike. She still went out with him for lunch about every other day. From the things Gary said to Bryan and Rick upon his return, he knew Shannon had omitted parts of the conversation when she recounted to him what was said. Not that she owed him an explanation. What she did and whom she chose to spend her time with was her decision. Regardless of how it hurt. "If you don't mind, I don't want to talk about it."

"Neither do I," she replied tersely.

Todd clenched his teeth, then began to pat his pockets, making it look as if he couldn't find something. "I'll be right back. Or if you want, I'll meet you at my place. I have to go back inside for a minute."

Shannon sighed loudly. "Did you lose your keys again? We go through this same routine at least a couple of times a week. I think I'm going to buy you one of those key-chain things with a voice-activated signal."

He knew she thought he was a birdbrain, but if Shannon left at the same time he did, he wouldn't get a chance to slip a new note in her drawer. She had started coming to work earlier in the morning, so he was no longer certain he would arrive before her. He had to make sure he left each new note when he went home at the end of the day.

"Very funny," he grumbled, trying to make it sound as if he was annoyed. "I'll be right back."

No one was in the main office when he returned, making his mission fast and efficient. He was back in the parking lot at the same time Shannon's car pulled up to the exit. While she waited for an opening in the traffic, she turned around, so he held his keys in the air and waved. She waved back to acknowledge that he had them, then turned back to the traffic and pulled out as soon as she had an opening.

Todd hurried home, arriving only a minute behind her. She left her car in the visitor parking and hopped into his car to go to the supermarket, where he pretended he knew what she bought, when he had no clue what some of the strange things were called. Soon they were in his kitchen, ready to start cooking. She showed him how to cut the chicken into small pieces and cook it. Then they added cut-up vegetables while the noodles cooked in another pot.

"This would go so much easier if you had a wok."

"I'm lucky to have this big frying pan. I just bought it a couple of weeks ago. I found it at a garage sale. I didn't know this was going to be such a complicated thing with so much to do."

"You said you wanted to make something that was mostly vegetables."

Todd lifted the lid to the pan and tested a noodle to see

if it was cooked. "I know. My mother doesn't eat enough vegetables."

Shannon smiled. "Usually, it's the other way around. Mothers telling their sons they don't eat enough vegetables."

Todd didn't reply. Instead, he grunted so she would think he'd said something.

"How's your mother doing anyway? My mom was asking about her again. Lately, I've been seeing you more than Craig. In fact, I don't think you've done anything with Craig for a week, since he's been seeing so much of Faye. So Mom asked me instead of Craig to ask you about your mom."

"She's doing better," he mumbled.

"I'm sorry. I didn't know she was sick. You never talk about your mom."

"There isn't much to say," he muttered as he replaced the lid. "I don't think these are done yet."

He flinched as Shannon's fingers rested on his arm. Todd looked first at Shannon's hand on his arm, then up at her face to see the saddest expression he'd ever seen.

"I don't know what's wrong with your mom. My mom has been asking me about her ever since we've been working together, so I know it's not that she had the flu or something temporary. Todd, please tell me what's wrong."

"It's nothing."

Her grip tightened for a second as she gave his arm a gentle squeeze. "Maybe there's something I can do."

He stiffened. "There's nothing you can do. There's nothing anyone can do. Except Mom. When she decides herself."

Todd lifted the lid again and watched the noodles in the boiling water. Even though he doubted much had changed in the last thirty seconds, he poked at them with the fork, about to taste another noodle, which forced Shannon to release his arm.

He didn't want to talk to Shannon about his mother. Only

a few people knew besides the social worker. Craig knew everything, but he'd said a few tidbits to Craig's mother in a moment of weakness. At the time, it felt good to get some of it off his chest; but later, he regretted saying anything because she kept asking how things were going, and he never had anything good to report. The only other person who knew what was going on was his pastor, and Todd planned to keep it that way.

In his peripheral vision, he saw Shannon shuffle around so she was behind him. He was about to scoop up another noodle when Shannon's arms slipped around his waist. He nearly dropped both the fork and the lid when she held him tight and pressed her cheek into his back between his shoulder blades.

"Come on, Todd. You can talk to me. I want to help you. Can't I do more than help you cook? Even if there's nothing else I can do, I can pray for her."

He clenched his teeth. But when she started rubbing little circles on his arm with her hand, he felt as if he would fall apart. He nearly threw the fork and lid onto the counter so he could peel her off him. As he covered her hand with his own, Shannon sighed. The heat of her breath through his shirt warmed a spot below his shoulder blade, and the movement of the sigh pressed her closer to him. Instead of pulling her hands off, he found himself holding them tighter, just to keep her there.

"You can tell me," she whispered against his back. "That's what friends are for."

Friends. Todd squeezed his eyes shut. He wanted so much more. Lately, he'd had dreams of spending his life with Shannon, not just at work, but living together as man and wife, with a dozen kids in a cozy, stable little house with a white picket fence and a big black dog in the backyard. Instead, Shannon was spending more time with Gary.

Todd had planned to talk to her today about Gary while

they were cooking, although they were nearly finished and he still hadn't thought of a way to put his thoughts into words. He knew she liked Gary. But Todd couldn't tell her everything, especially how Gary threatened his job. Regardless of how she felt about Gary, if he told her what Gary had said, she was bound to say something to him that would get both of them fired. That would end the relationship, but Todd didn't want Shannon to lose her job because of something he'd started. He needed to think of a better way. He couldn't think properly with Shannon wrapped around him, though. But he didn't want her to be anywhere else.

Todd forced his thoughts away from Gary and back to what they were talking about earlier—his mother.

He tried to clear his throat, but his voice came out in a hoarse croak. "No one can help. She's been like this since my dad left when I was in my teens. I help her a little bit with the basics when she comes over for dinner on Tuesdays, and I go through her stuff."

"Go through her stuff? I don't understand." Todd's head swam. He chose his words carefully. "She's never been good with money or anything that required any planning or advance preparation. She doesn't take care of herself, and she's not good with commitments, but she will come here every Tuesday for dinner and for me to balance her checkbook. That's why I want to feed her something with lots of vegetables. It's the only good meal she gets all week."

Shannon's hands didn't move beneath his, but she gave him a short, gentle squeeze. "I can't imagine anyone cooking any worse than you do. Between you and Craig, I remember a few disasters in my mom's kitchen. But that's so sweet. Do you give her leftovers to take home?"

"Yes, but she eats everything when she gets home, and the next day it's back to the usual patterns."

He felt her arms stiffen. Part of him wanted her never to

let him go, but the more sensible part of him told him to pick up her hands and push her away. Having Shannon's arms around him had altered his judgment, and he'd already said more than he should have.

"Usual patterns? What usual patterns?"

She gave him another gentle squeeze. All Todd's self-constraint melted away. He pressed his hands more firmly over hers, as if the closer contact could make everything better.

"On payday, if she's working, she blows all her money on stupid things—cigarettes, movies, clothes, things she doesn't need. I know a lot of the money goes toward illegal drugs, but I can never catch her with them. And then she has nothing. Often she can't pay the rent, and the landlord threatens to evict her. That's one reason why I go through her checkbook. I don't give her money because she'll spend it, then not tell me what she did with it. So I pay her landlord myself. I also give her groceries, but sometimes she sells them for much less than I paid for them, just to get a couple of dollars for more drugs. When she's completely out of food and money, I make her come here, and I feed her. When she's hungry enough, she comes, even if it isn't Tuesday."

Shannon squeezed him tighter. "I'm so sorry. I didn't know. Isn't there anything you can do? Can't social assistance help her? Or a counselor at church or something? There are agencies and all sorts of places she can go to for help."

Todd remained silent while he tried to maintain his composure, grateful Shannon was behind him and couldn't see his face. He did feel awkward talking to her this way, though it was easier. He'd talked to his mother's social worker and his pastor more times than he could count. As an adult, he understood more of her mental state than before, but in his teen years, he hadn't known what was wrong or what he could do about it. He only knew that none of his friends lived the way he did.

Craig had been the only one to see through the show he

put on for the rest of the world. Todd had confided in him, especially when matters got bad and his mother started selling his belongings when he wasn't home. Whenever he confronted her about his things being missing, especially treasured or high-priced items, she either yelled at him or slapped him for accusing her of stealing.

Since she was his mother, he certainly couldn't hit her back, even when she went berserk and hit him repeatedly. Once, he remembered breaking down in front of Craig when he asked him how things were going. That was when Craig had involved his pastor, but his mother only got worse and kicked him out. It was the worst thing she could have done for herself, but perhaps it was best for Todd. By then, he couldn't do anything more, and it gave him the separation he needed. He'd been an adult then and already supporting her for the most part for years. Now he helped her from a distance, when she was desperate enough to accept it.

Todd stiffened as he repeated the words he'd heard so often and was helpless to do anything about. "She's not breaking into homes and stealing things, and she's not really hurting anyone but herself with everything else, so they say there's nothing anyone can do until she makes the decision to get help herself. My only choices are to have her arrested or committed. I can't do either one. She hasn't stolen from anyone else besides me, at least not that I know of. I'm certainly not going to press charges. Even if I did, they wouldn't lock up a first-time offender. And she's not whacked out enough to be placed in a rehabilitation center without her consent. All I can do is be there to pick up the pieces and make sure she has a roof over her head."

Shannon pulled her hands away, releasing her backward hug, and stepped back. He didn't intend to move, but she latched onto his arm and turned him around until they stood face-to-face, leaving her hand on his arm. "I had no idea things were that bad. Why didn't you tell me?"

The pain in her eyes touched him deeply. The last thing he wanted was her sympathy. He was coping with everything—badly at times—but with help from the Lord, he was coping better than before.

Todd wanted to hold her tight, but he knew if she wrapped her arms around him again he would fall apart, and he couldn't let that happen. Instead, he smiled wryly and brushed a wayward lock of hair out of her eyes so he had something to do with his other hand. "We never had that kind of relationship."

"I guess. I'm beginning to see I didn't know you at all and am only starting to get to know you."

Todd didn't know if that was good or bad, so he chose not to comment. "I think the noodles are probably wrecked by now. I guess my cooking skills haven't improved over the years."

"Forget the noodles. I think you need a hug."

Without waiting for him to respond, she stepped forward and pressed herself into him. She slid her hands around his back and held him tight.

Todd couldn't have spoken if the roof had caved in. His heart pounded, his eyes burned, and he could barely breathe. He'd never thought of hugging as an answer, but she was right. Holding Shannon didn't solve anything, but he did feel better, and he had never loved her more.

Shannon spoke first. "Maybe we should check those noodles, before they burn in the bottom of the pan." She moved away from him.

He ached from the separation, but he didn't want to wreck his only good pan.

Shannon stepped in front of him, took a clean fork out of the drawer, and pulled a noodle out. Watching her pucker up and blow on the steaming noodle made Todd think of her puckering up for something much better than eating. When she blew on the noodle a second time, it almost hurt not to kiss her.

She slurped the noodle into her mouth and chewed it thoughtfully. "A little overdone, but not terminal." She turned off the heat and removed the pan from the stove top. "They're fine if we eat right now. You set the table, and I'll drain them and mix everything together."

Todd scrambled to set the table. They said a short prayer of thanks and began to eat.

Todd ate a mouthful, then swirled some of the noodles with his fork. "I've been meaning to ask you something. About your Secret Admirer. Do you have any ideas?"

She laid her fork down. "Yes and no. Sometimes I think I know for sure it's Gary, then other times I don't think he's the one at all. Why do you ask?"

Todd tried to appear neutral. "I was just wondering how you feel about Gary."

"I'm not sure yet. Sometimes I have my doubts about his sincerity, but other times, I think he's struggling with something. I know what he's like with the ladies." She gave a little giggle, suddenly dampening Todd's optimism that she had seen through Gary's ploys. "But I can't help it. He's a lot of fun, and I think that when he decides to settle down, he'll make some woman a wonderful husband."

Todd's hopes sank. He knew he was lousy husband material. For all his hopes and dreams, his own home was as dysfunctional as they came. Before his father left, he had vivid memories of arguing and shouting. A few times his parents had resorted to throwing things at each other.

His only example on how to be a good husband, and even a good father, was Shannon and Craig's father. He loved and respected their parents immensely, but watching his own family had taught him the outside world rarely saw what went on behind closed doors. When it came down to the intimate workings of a relationship, he didn't know what to do.

Gary, on the other hand, knew exactly how to treat a

woman, because all the women loved him, despite what he said to the other men when no ladies were present. Yet maybe what Gary said to him, Bryan, and Rick was only a macho front. Maybe he really did know how to treat a woman right.

"Yeah," Todd mumbled, as he stuffed a forkful of vegetables and noodles into his mouth. "Good luck."

thirteen

Shannon listened to Todd's laughter, echoing from the dispatch office all the way to her desk. The sound made her smile, without even knowing what was so funny. She peeked over her shoulder, confirming he had the same effect on Brenda and Nanci, who were both grinning for no apparent reason as they worked.

In so many ways, Todd was as big a mystery as her Secret Admirer. She'd known Todd came from a single-parent family, and she'd known something was wrong; but she had no idea his situation was so tragic. When she returned home after having dinner with him a few days ago, she'd buried herself in prayer, first for Todd's mother, then for Todd. The night they'd talked, she'd even shed a few tears for Todd. She'd prayed for him daily since then.

Knowing now what she didn't know before, she had to give Todd credit. Despite his hardships and heartaches, he had a marvelous sense of humor—maybe that's what had saved his sanity over the years. He sometimes overdid it, but he was honorable and sincere, two traits she valued. She'd always known his heart was in the right place, even before he accepted the sacrifice of Christ in his life.

For all he'd been through, he was remarkably well adjusted. He also handled his money well, if he covered his own living expenses, plus most of his mother's rent nearly every month. His actions also proved a kind and generous spirit. If the same thing had happened to others, most people would have simply left and not looked back. Not only was Todd taking care of his mother as much as she allowed him, he was also covering a large expense knowing he had no chance of repayment or even being appreciated.

This was the problem Craig wouldn't tell her about years before. She suspected Todd's pastor was aware of it, but she doubted anyone else was except her. And she knew only because she'd pried it out of him.

Others would have called him a sucker. Shannon thought he was a saint. She had underestimated him. Previously she thought Gary would have made some woman a wonderful husband, but she had revised that opinion. Gary was too self-centered and full of his own accomplishments and ego to be a good life's partner, at least for her. Todd, on the other hand, was everything she had ever dreamed of in a man. If she wasn't sure before, she was now. She didn't know exactly when it happened, but she'd fallen hopelessly in love with Todd Sanders.

But Todd only wanted to be friends. He'd told her so on more than one occasion. And she couldn't blame him. She was, after all, his best friend's kid sister. Regardless of her age, in his eyes, she would always be Craig's kid sister.

If being friends was the best she could be, then she had to accept that. Although it was only a teenage crush at the time, she had been in love with him before and lived through it. If all Todd wanted to be was friends, then being friends was better than not being friends.

Shannon glanced up at the clock. It was still hours before lunch break, but she could hardly wait. Not that she was hungry. Since Gary had a meeting with a client, she would be staying in the lunchroom and taking her break with Todd today.

At the thought of spending some time with Todd, whether or not anyone else joined them at the table, Shannon began to hum as she picked up her stapler and the statistical report for the graveyard shift's productivity. When she tried to staple the report together, she discovered her stapler was empty. She pulled the drawer open and groped for the box of staples, but instead, her fingers brushed the newest note from the Secret Admirer, which she'd left in her drawer instead of tucking it in the envelope in her filing cabinet.

Shannon glanced from side to side to make sure no one was watching. Ignoring her empty stapler, she picked up the note and read it for probably the fifth time that day.

Dearest Shannon,
  Of all the things that make life worthwhile
  Nothing makes me happier than your lovely smile.
  You're bonded to my heart, as steadfast as with glue,
  And that's why I write these words of love to you.
                                              Your Secret Admirer

Usually, she didn't reread the notes until she got home, but this one she did. Not that it was better than the others; in fact this one seemed worse. The theme was still sweet and the message touching, but in this one, the pentameter seemed more off than usual, which made her think of all the notes and how they were constructed.

Gary had hinted he was the Secret Admirer, but he was a gifted speaker. His vocabulary was better than the words used in the notes, which she'd been studying at home. She had also discovered a pattern. The most elaborate words were those at the ends of the sentences, the words that rhymed, which didn't make sense. In today's note, however, she'd found an exception.

The word "steadfast" was a word she'd never heard anyone use in normal conversation. In fact, the only place she'd heard the word was at church.

Gary didn't go to church. Or rather he did, but that had only been for the past month. If Shannon were honest with herself, she wasn't sure how much he paid attention. She certainly didn't think he paid attention enough to make a word like "steadfast" part of his everyday vocabulary, especially in what was supposed to be a love sonnet.

After a month, she was starting to have some serious doubts about Gary's alleged interest in Christianity. She'd given him a Bible and pointed out some key verses for him to read, but every time she questioned him, he avoided answering or made an excuse about why he hadn't read that section. She now suspected he hadn't read a single passage she'd suggested.

At the sound of a chair scraping behind her, Shannon stuck the note in her pocket and picked up the box of staples from the drawer. She had almost finished tucking the row of staples into the slot when Rick walked through the doorway from the dispatch office and handed her an envelope.

"Kyle said to give this to you."

As she always did when she received something handwritten, she studied the writing, especially when the person wrote her name. She could easily compare the letter *S* from *Shannon* to the signature *Secret Admirer*.

Kyle on the north city route was not the Secret Admirer.

She quickly read the letter, which was Kyle's request to take a few days off and get his vacation pay. Even though he'd done it correctly by making his request in writing, he'd missed a step. Before she paid him, Kyle had to get permission from the department head to take the time off.

Letter in hand, she walked into Gary's office.

Gary read the letter quickly, called up the staffing schedule on the computer, then nodded. "Sure. He can have those days. I have a couple of guys on the casual list who aren't working and would be happy to get some hours."

Shannon started to turn around, but Gary spoke again.

"Shannon, do you have a minute? I'd like to talk to you about something."

She turned around and sank into one of the plush chairs in front of Gary's desk. "Yes?"

"I was wondering if you'd like to join me for dinner tonight." He quickly held up his hands to stop her from turning him down instantly. "I know what you're going to say, but this is different. I just received an e-mail from the customer I'm going to be joining for lunch, and he's given me a couple of tickets to the theater. They're for tonight, which doesn't give me a lot of time to ask someone properly. I know it's not much notice, but you'd be doing me a favor. I have to go because it's a business obligation rather than something I want to do, and you'd save me from going alone." Gary paused and flashed her a heart-stopping smile. "If you want to justify this, you can call it work-related."

"I don't know. May I think about it before I give you my answer?"

"Of course. But I'd appreciate it if you let me know as soon as possible. And while we're out, I think it would be a good time to tell you about a little"—Gary dropped his voice to an alluring whisper—"secret."

Shannon's heart began to pound. She gulped, trying to make her voice sound normal. "What kind of secret?"

He leaned forward over the desk, not losing the smile Shannon knew melted women's hearts by the dozen. "If I told you now, then it wouldn't be a secret, would it?"

"I suppose not," she choked out.

"I've always *admired* a well-kept *secret*, haven't you?"

Shannon forced herself to breathe. She sprang to her feet. "I'll let you know about dinner after lunch." Before Gary could pressure her, Shannon left his office and returned to her desk.

A million thoughts zinged through her head. She didn't know what Gary was going to say, but she wasn't stupid. She could tell he was alluding to the Secret Admirer. Just because he knew, though, didn't mean he was the Secret Admirer.

Faye knew, Todd knew, and she suspected Nanci did, too. She also had the impression Rick knew, because he worked closely with Todd and might have overheard them talking about it a couple of times.

Regardless of who knew, since the time she started receiving the notes, she was no closer to discovering the man's identity. The only thing that had happened was that she had gained three pounds. She attributed part of that to going out with Todd for coffee and dessert twice a week, but part of it also had to be a steady diet of a chocolate kiss every morning.

Shannon glanced at the clock. Little time had passed since she'd last checked, but now she wanted it to be the lunch hour more than ever. She hadn't talked much about the Secret Admirer with anyone, but this time, she had to. She had to know if it was Gary, and if it took going out with him in the evening to get an answer, then that was what she would have to do.

But first, she had to discuss it with Todd.

To make sure Todd didn't forget she was remaining in the building for lunch, Shannon returned to the dispatch area, staying clear of Gary's office door.

She found Todd alone in the room, not working, standing and staring out the window.

"Hey, Todd. Working hard, I see." She couldn't help but grin. "What's so interesting out there?"

He smiled. "I was just looking at the spring sunshine. See how it sparkles?"

Shannon grinned wider. Sunshine may be bright, but she'd never seen sunshine sparkle. Only Todd would think of something so strange.

She stepped beside him, so she was looking out the same window. "It's bright and sunny out there, a nice spring day. But I don't see any sparkles."

He wrapped his hands around her shoulders and turned her in the direction of the trees in the corner of the parking lot. "I'm not talking about the glitter type of sparkles that kids use for their arts and crafts projects. Look." He pointed directly at the trees. "It stopped raining, and the sun came out right away. Everything is still wet. See how the sunshine catches the raindrops on the leaves? And see how the droplets of water shine on that big spider web? Do you see it? It's kind of like dew on the grass early in the morning, but the sun isn't bright enough at sunrise to make the dew sparkle. It's well past sunrise now, though, so the rain is drying fast. The sparkling spring sunshine happens only early in the day, when the weather is cool but not too cold, for that few minutes while everything is wet after a quick rain. Like today. It lasts a minute or two, if the angle of the sunlight is right, and then it's gone. Kind of like the commercial for those chocolate Easter eggs. They last only a short time, and then they're gone until next year. That's what makes it so special. It fascinates me every time, because it's unique and pretty. And now, I better get back to work."

Shannon looked outside at the tree, but she didn't see anything. Her mind was elsewhere.

Sparkling spring sunshine. She'd heard the phrase before.

One of the Secret Admirer's poems had used that phrase. She didn't memorize the poems, or even parts of them, but that one phrase had caught her attention at the time because it was so odd.

Todd had just said the same phrase.

It was Todd. Todd Sanders was the Secret Admirer. She pressed her hand over the top of her pocket with the Secret Admirer's latest note in it.

Todd's latest note.

Todd Sanders was the man who had been writing words of love to her, as today's poem had professed.

She turned to watch Todd busily typing at the computer, hard at work.

"Todd?"

He turned around, smiling. His eyes sparkled, just like his spring sunshine. "Yes?"

Behind her, footsteps approached, meaning either Bryan or Rick or both were returning. Gary's phone was ringing in his office. One of the dispatch phones started ringing, and a beeping and flashing light signaled that one of the drivers was calling in. It was payback time for the three minutes of silence.

This was not the time to tell him she knew.

Shannon cleared her throat, hoping she could make her voice sound normal. "I just wanted to see if we're on for lunch together, since I'm not going out."

He picked up the phone. "You betcha." He pushed the button to get the caller. "Dispatch. This is Todd."

Bryan appeared and reached for the radio. Rick started walking into Gary's office with a folder, but Gary met him halfway, and they both stepped into the dispatch area.

Without a word Shannon turned and returned to her desk, but she didn't sit down. Immediately, she removed the key to her filing cabinet from her pocket. Her hands shook so badly she didn't know how she got the key into the lock. She reached for Todd's personnel file. For all the years she'd known him, she'd never seen his handwriting. When the Secret Admirer notes started appearing, she'd checked the handwriting of a few of the men, but it never occurred to her to look at Todd's.

Shannon pulled out the tax form he'd filled out and studied Todd's signature at the bottom.

The S in Sanders was a perfect match.

The last note she'd read flashed through her mind. This time, instead of reading a message from a piece of paper, she imagined Todd's voice saying the words.

> *"You're bonded to my heart, as steadfast as with glue,*
> *And that's why I write these words of love to you."*

"Oh. . .Todd. . . ," she whispered.

She replaced everything, locked the cabinet, and resumed her work. By the time her lunch break finally arrived, her stomach felt so fluttery she didn't know if she could eat.

Todd was his usual smiling self as he sat at the table in the lunchroom, waiting for her, the contents of his lunch tote already spread out.

Shannon quickly retrieved her lunch from the fridge and joined him.

So he couldn't see her hands shaking, Shannon didn't open her lunch but instead folded her hands in her lap. "Before we eat, I was wondering, is there anything you'd like to tell me? Something important?"

He opened one of his containers, removed a sandwich, and rested it on the lid.

"Not really. Give me a hint."

"Something that might be a secret?"

His eyes widened, and his smile dropped for a split second, but he recovered quickly. He rested his hands on the tabletop and leaned forward. "I hear everyone's going out for dinner next month, and one of the birthdays for the month is yours. Faye asked me to buy a card."

"That's not a secret."

He straightened, and his grin widened. "Sorry. That's the best I can do. If you want juicy gossip, you have to go elsewhere."

She realized he wouldn't tell her unless she forced it out of him so she tried to think of how she could reword her thoughts in a way that would pin Todd into a corner.

He sat there, staring at her, not eating, making her realize it was her turn to say grace. She led in a short prayer of thanks for their food, and they began to eat.

She thought she'd try again, perhaps coming at the issue another way. "I was wondering. Have you ever thought about—"

Todd's foot tapped hers under the table, halting her words. "Hey! Faye! What do you say?" Todd quipped while looking over Shannon's shoulder. Faye slid into the empty chair beside Shannon. After she was settled, Todd grinned at her. "Have a seat. Why don't you join us?"

Shannon couldn't help but smile, as did Faye.

Faye plunked a notepad on the table in front of her and focused her attention on Todd. "Someone suggested that you should be on the social committee. We're going to start making plans for the Christmas party next meeting, and Nanci and Brenda think you should be there."

Todd blinked. "Christmas? But it's only May."

"If we want to book the banquet room we like best, we have to do it soon. You wouldn't believe how fast the good places go."

"But I've never done anything like that before."

Shannon knew Todd would be good at administration.

"Oh, look," Faye said. "Here come Nanci and Brenda." She waved the duo over to the table. "Guess what? Todd said he's going to be on the social committee with us."

"I did?"

Both ladies winked at Todd as they slid into the last empty chairs at the table.

Shannon smiled. It appeared Todd's fate was sealed, with or without his approval.

Faye giggled. "I think this year the social committee stuff is going to be fun."

Rick also appeared. He pulled out a chair from another table, squeezed it in between Faye and Nanci and joined them. "Did someone mention the social committee?" He turned to Todd. "Did they volunteer you? Faye said she was going to ask. And I know how Faye 'asks.'"

With the sudden appearance of the entire social committee

at the table, Shannon had a feeling she wouldn't have the chance to talk to Todd without an audience.

Suddenly, Gary's voice sounded from behind her. "Rick, I've been looking for you. I need your report on John's accident. Sorry to bug you on your lunch break, but the insurance people need me to fax it to them by one o'clock, and I have to leave in five minutes to meet a client."

Shannon didn't look at Rick. While Gary was speaking, she watched Todd. She had told him about Gary's insinuations that he himself was the Secret Admirer. She could only guess now at how he felt. He had tried to get her to reconsider spending time with Gary for more than the fact he didn't like the man. It was because Todd knew the truth.

She clenched her fists under the table. Before she started receiving the Secret Admirer's notes, she had turned Gary down many times when he'd asked her for a date. She didn't know what he had planned for after attending the theater, but when she'd also been hesitant about that, even after he called it a business function, he'd insinuated he was going to tell her he was her Secret Admirer. By trying to make her believe he was the Secret Admirer when he wasn't, Gary was lying to her. Worse than lying, he was trying to take advantage of her, knowing she was in an emotionally vulnerable state.

She had no idea why he was trying so hard. But Gary didn't care about the hearts he broke. Jody was still nursing her wounded heart and had been for six months. He hadn't been interested in a relationship with Jody; he only wanted to have fun with her. Shannon wasn't interested in that type of relationship. She didn't want love or loyalty from Gary. She wanted his honesty, which she knew she wasn't getting. If he cared about her, he wouldn't lie to her. He wanted something else—probably the same thing he got from Jody—and Shannon wasn't giving that to him.

Apparently, Gary was using any means he could to break

her down. After more than a month of leading her to believe
he was interested in God, he hadn't read anything from the
Bible she'd given him. Nor had Gary ever had any appropriate questions or comments on the pastor's sermons. Looking
back, she doubted he was even paying attention to the pastor's words. Gary was using her desire to share her faith and
attending church with her as another ploy to make her fall
into his clutches.

Todd was right. She was completely out of her league with
Gary. She didn't want to think of what would happen if she
went out with him. If she had to imagine the worst that
could happen, it would be her word against his, when she
had voluntarily spent so much time with him over the past
month, with many witnesses to bear testimony to the fact
that she was a willing victim.

To allude to being the Secret Admirer was deceitful
enough, but going to church under false pretenses intending
to take advantage of her was reprehensible.

Slowly, Shannon turned around. After what she'd just
thought of as a worst-case scenario if she did see Gary on her
own time, what she was going to say was best stated in front
of witnesses. "Gary, about our earlier conversation. I've
decided not to go out with you this evening. You'll have to
find someone else to schmooze the customers with you. In
fact, I think it would be a good idea if we didn't see each
other on weekends anymore, either. And that includes Sunday
mornings."

Gary's smile faltered for a second, but he recovered quickly,
putting on a great macho show in front of the other ladies.
"You don't know what you're missing." He lowered his voice
to a playful growl. "We'd have been good together."

After everything she'd been thinking, the concept of being
coupled with Gary made her stomach churn. "I don't think
so. I don't appreciate the way you've been trying to get me to

believe something you know isn't true. I think it best if we only see each other at work, during working hours. And that includes lunch. Effective immediately."

Gary grinned and shrugged his shoulders. "It's all in the game." He glanced around the table at everyone sitting there, most noticeably Rick and Todd, as two single men who could supposedly relate. "Win some, lose some. Rick, I need that report. I have to get back because I have to leave."

Rick stood and walked back to the dispatch area with Gary.

Shannon felt as if she'd been stabbed. She wasn't playing games. She'd been serious about the time she'd spent with Gary, hoping for results and praying for his eternal salvation. She'd risked her friendship with Todd, knowing Todd disapproved; yet she'd gone ahead with her plans to minister to Gary anyway. All she wanted was for Gary to respect her faith and accept Jesus as his Savior. If not, she at least hoped to be friends so the door would be open for the future, when he was ready. She certainly hadn't expected to be brushed off like a toy he no longer had any hope of playing with.

She'd never felt so insulted in her life.

With Gary and Rick out of the room, Nanci turned to Shannon and giggled. "Good one, Shan. It serves him right for how he treated Jody. Score one for us girls!"

If Shannon had any remnants of her appetite left after talking to Gary, she had absolutely zero desire to eat now. She wasn't out to hurt people to avenge past wrongs, nor did she have any inclination to play gender battles. She also didn't want to talk to Todd about the Secret Admirer anymore. She couldn't look him in the face, not knowing if she'd see sympathy, anger, or pity in his eyes.

She just wanted to be alone.

Shannon snapped the lid back on her salad bowl. "I guess I wasn't as hungry as I thought. I'll catch you later." Since she didn't have anything else to do, Shannon returned to her desk ten minutes early and resumed her work. If she couldn't be alone, keeping busy was probably best, which was easy while she was at work.

At the end of the workday, she could go home and lick her wounds. She wasn't in a position to quit her job over a personal injury, and she knew Gary wouldn't, either. In fact, Gary probably didn't even consider her rejection of him an injury. He'd brushed off Jody, and Jody was madly in love with him. In Gary's mind, Shannon was nothing, which on top of everything else added insult to injury with her bruised ego.

Tomorrow, after spending some time alone with God and getting a good night's sleep, she knew she would feel somewhat better, and life could go on as normal.

But until then she had work to do.

fourteen

"I can have the driver back there in twenty minutes. . . . You're welcome." Todd hung up the phone and paged the driver in question, but his mind was elsewhere. No matter how busy he was, he couldn't stop thinking about Shannon.

To the best of Todd's knowledge, only Faye knew about the Secret Admirer. Rick knew something was going on, but he didn't know what. He didn't think anyone else knew besides Gary, and that was because Gary had been snooping in Shannon's desk. From the way Shannon had worded her statement to Gary, no one except those who knew about the Secret Admirer would have been able to figure out the meaning of her words.

Somehow, since the last time he'd spoken to her about it, Shannon had determined the Secret Admirer wasn't Gary. Todd was more relieved than words could express that Shannon had decided not to see Gary outside of work. Last night, he'd hardly slept at all. He'd decided that, even if Shannon didn't want to save herself, Todd would. Whether or not it put him at risk of being fired, Todd had decided to confront Gary and put a stop to his pursuit of Shannon at the close of work Friday, which was that day. Now it appeared she had solved the problem herself, in the nick of time, without any input or help from him.

Of course he was relieved. And though the result was what he wanted, Todd didn't like the way Gary brushed off Shannon in front of everyone. Maybe he'd done it to cover up his own embarrassment, but he didn't need to wound her in the process. She tried to hide it, but he could see she was hurt because she couldn't even finish her lunch.

Todd wished he could do something about it, but there was nothing he could do or say except for giving her a few platitudes. For all the time he'd spent with her, and in all his efforts to treat her special, Shannon only thought of him as a friend and nothing more. He would have approached her on bended knee to propose love and marriage if he thought it would have helped. But he'd been on bended knee once before, singing Happy Birthday at the top of his lungs in the middle of a crowded restaurant to get her a free piece of cake. She didn't take him seriously then; she wouldn't take him seriously this time, even if he meant it from the bottom of his heart.

Last night he'd also thought about revealing himself as the Secret Admirer after the close of work today, whether or not he was still employed. That plan had also been squelched. After Gary treated her as little better than a piece of fluff in front of her work friends, she needed the Secret Admirer to hold her up and tell her how special she was more than ever. If she found out now that he was the Secret Admirer, the joy she'd received from the notes would only be a disappointment.

As the day continued, the phones eventually quieted down, and most of the drivers were told to start coming in as everything began to wind down for the close of business. Todd took advantage of a rare moment of silence to go to the supply closet for a computer disk to back up his work for the day.

When he walked into the closet, it suddenly dawned on him how quiet it was and how alone he was.

No one was in the closet except him and God.

Todd closed his eyes and prayed. He thanked God for Shannon's friendship, for the improvement in their relationship, and that she had put the past behind them. He praised

God that Gary hadn't made a big scene or thrown his corporate weight around. After lunch, everything had gone on as usual, indicating no harm had been done, except the pain in Shannon's heart. He prayed for God to show him a way to help her deal with it, even if it meant continuing to be her Secret Admirer and hold her up. It wasn't what he wanted to do; but if that was what Shannon needed right now, then he would do it.

He wasn't quite finished when he heard someone coming. He opened his eyes, reached onto the shelf, and wrapped his fingers around a new disk just as Faye stepped into the closet.

She squeaked when she saw him. "Todd! You scared me!"

He scrambled to clear his thoughts, turned around, disk in hand, and grinned impishly. "Boo."

Faye giggled. "It's almost time to go home now. I guess I'll see you Sunday at church. Craig wants to go out for lunch afterward. Will you be coming?"

Todd shrugged his shoulders. He didn't feel like watching Craig and Faye cuddle up to each other when he couldn't be doing the same with Shannon, who would be at her own church. Gary wouldn't be with her, but she hadn't asked Todd to join her, as he had hoped she would. The lack of an invitation told him everything he needed to know. "Not sure. I might just go home after the service. Three can sometimes be a crowd."

Her smile widened. "As much as I enjoy your company, I won't argue with you there. We'll see what happens."

Todd nodded and left the room to get back to his job, feeling more alone than he had for years.

⁂

Shannon glanced up at the clock. It was ten minutes past Todd's quitting time. Everyone in the main office had gone home, but Todd still hadn't appeared from the dispatch area.

If he wouldn't come to her, then she would go to him.

She found him bundling the last of the pickup sheets for the day. Bryan was on the phone, and Rick was leaning toward the opening to the drivers' area, talking to one of the casual drivers. Since Todd was the first person to start in the morning, he was first to go home while the others stayed to receive the paperwork from the drivers as they brought their shipments into the building for distribution.

Shannon stepped behind him as he bent over to toss the bundle into the box. "Are you ready to go, Todd?"

"Go? Go where?"

Shannon smiled. "Home, silly. Let's walk out to the parking lot together. Actually, I'm hungry because I didn't finish my lunch. How would you like to join me, and we'll go grab an early dinner someplace? I'll buy. There's something I need to talk to you about."

"I. . .uh. . ." Todd blinked, looked up at the clock, then back to her. "Sure."

Shannon waited until he tidied up his area, and they walked out of the building together.

Instead of laughing and telling jokes, Todd's mood was somber. They had reached his car before he finally spoke.

"I don't know if this is the right time or place to say this, but I'm going to say it anyway. I think you made the right decision about not seeing Gary anymore. If the day ever comes when he wants to search for God, he knows where to go and who to ask. I hope one day that will happen. I really do. In a way, I feel sorry for him. I don't know how he ever thought you wouldn't find out he was only leading you on. The big loser here is Gary, not you."

"Thanks. I appreciate your saying that." After thinking about Gary's rebuff, she'd come to terms with it quickly. Her ego was still bruised, but the big loser truly was Gary. Worse than turning down Shannon's offers of friendship, Gary had rejected God.

Todd reached to pull on the handle to his car door, which of course was locked. "Oops," he muttered.

Shannon smiled at what she knew was going to happen. She could have counted the seconds each stage took as he performed his routine.

Todd straightened and stuck his right hand in his right pocket. He pulled his hand out, empty, then stuck his left hand in his left pocket. Again, when he removed his hand, it was empty. He began to pat all his pockets, but Shannon knew his attempts to find his keys would be futile.

"I have to go back inside. Wait here for me. I'll be right back."

Shannon reached out to touch his arm, barely able to hold back her grin.

When he turned around and looked at her, Shannon had to nibble on her bottom lip in an effort to keep a straight face. "Why don't you check the back pocket of your jeans? I think you'll find your keys there."

Todd reached behind him and patted both back pockets with both hands. "Well. How about that? You're a genius."

She couldn't hold back her grin anymore. "Not really. But you're the one who's going to have to be a genius to figure out another excuse to go back inside the building while you leave me here outside. I've got you figured out. I know what you're doing."

Todd's face paled instantly. He froze with his hands still covering his back pockets.

"Every time you've gone back inside for your keys, you've known where they were. Your keys weren't the issue. You've gone back to my desk when you knew I wouldn't see what you were doing."

"But. . ." Todd's voice trailed off.

Shannon reached forward and rested her hands on his arms and looked up into his eyes. Eyes that showed so many things—now his hesitation and uncertainty. Above all, his eyes showed depth of character—a man who was sweet and sensitive, despite the display of bravado he put on for the rest of the world. She mentally kicked herself for taking so long to see it.

Her voice dropped to a whisper. "It's you. It's been you all along."

Todd looked down at her hands. He stood, frozen, not moving a muscle. "I. . ." His voice trailed off again.

Shannon shuffled closer, not caring if anyone else they worked with saw them. "You might as well give me the note right here instead of making me wait until morning." Leaving her left hand still on his arm, she reached into her own pocket and withdrew a piece of paper. "But first, this is for you."

Todd accepted the paper from her hand. "What's this?"

"It's a note, silly. Read it."

Todd's hand was shaking as he read what she'd written.

Dearest Secret Admirer,
  I have no chocolate kiss to share
  All I have are my words and a prayer.
  It's been hard to rhyme when my mind meanders
  Because I'm in love with you, too, Todd Sanders.
                    Yours forever, Shannon

Todd stared at the note, read it a second time, and gulped. "I'm speechless." Still clutching the paper, he brushed his fingers against her cheek and looked deep into her eyes.

The parking lot, the vans, the traffic on the street behind her—the whole world around her faded into oblivion. Todd's beautiful brown eyes were warm and inviting and as sweet as the chocolate he had given her every day.

He cleared his throat, but his voice still came out so low and husky she could barely understand him. "Do you mean this?"

Shannon's heart pounded so hard she wondered if he could hear it. "As much as you've meant your notes to me."

He cupped both her cheeks with his palms. "I love you so much that words are inadequate."

Shannon started to open her mouth to respond, but before she could speak, Todd's mouth covered hers. He kissed her passionately but still cupped her cheeks gently, using no force to keep her there except for her own compelling need to kiss him back. His gentle touch emphasized that his kiss came entirely from his heart and that he truly loved her as much as his notes had said.

Shannon slipped her arms around him to embrace him fully. She kissed him the same way he was kissing her, because she loved him, too.

"Woo hoo! Go, Todd!" a male voice called out from somewhere in the parking lot. From the other side of the lot, a horn honked.

Todd drew back slightly, his face red. "I guess the drivers are starting to come in. We should go someplace else. You said something about supper?"

Shannon knew her own face had to be as red as Todd's. "Yes. Where do you want to go?"

He brushed a light but lingering kiss on her lips, then released her completely. "I don't know. I'm so mixed up right now I can't think. I want to go someplace quiet and romantic so I can ask you to marry me, but it's probably too soon for that."

Shannon giggled. "I don't know about that, but if you wanted that tidbit to be a secret, you blew it. Now I won't answer until you ask me properly."

His cheeks flushed again. "Oops." They walked in silence to her car. Todd spoke as Shannon inserted the key into the lock.

"It's not very romantic, especially since we're taking separate cars, but there's a great place to eat not far from my apartment. It's called Joe's Diner. It's small, and it isn't fancy, but the food's great. The owners just got married, and the local paper said they've decorated the place like a wedding. The bride is wearing her veil all week, the groom is wearing a top hat, and the waiters and waitresses are wearing their wedding gear. They're also offering dinners for two at half price and giving away free cake, like wedding cake, to everyone for dessert."

"That sounds like your kind of place. I'll meet you there."

Shannon was so happy she felt lightheaded. As strange as it sounded, she couldn't think of a more romantic atmosphere for Todd to propose than in the midst of wedding decorations, even if the recent bride and groom were serving hamburgers. She could hardly wait to give him her answer.

Shannon pulled the car door open.

"Wait."

Before she could slide in, Todd's hands slipped around her waist. She turned around and rested her hands on his waist as well. They were hugging loosely, so that no one they worked with would tease or interrupt them.

Todd brushed a kiss on her temple, backed up a little but didn't release her. "I have to tell you this now, or I'll forget. That was a good poem you wrote, especially in a short time."

Shannon felt her face grow warm at his compliment. "Thanks. I found out writing poetry isn't easy. Do you know how difficult it was to think of something that rhymed with Sanders?"

Todd grinned, stepped back, covered his heart with his hand, and cleared his throat.

"Finding rhymes is easy when you know where to look. All it takes is to love a special woman, and then go buy a book."

A Letter To Our Readers

Dear Reader:

In order that we might better contribute to your reading enjoyment, we would appreciate your taking a few minutes to respond to the following questions. We welcome your comments and read each form and letter we receive. When completed, please return to the following:

Fiction Editor
Heartsong Presents
PO Box 719
Uhrichsville, Ohio 44683

1. Did you enjoy reading *Secret Admirer* by Gail Sattler?
   ❏ Very much! I would like to see more books by this author!
   ❏ Moderately. I would have enjoyed it more if

   _____

   _____

   _____

2. Are you a member of **Heartsong Presents**? ❏ Yes ❏ No
   If no, where did you purchase this book? _____

   _____

3. How would you rate, on a scale from 1 (poor) to 5 (superior), the cover design? _____

4. On a scale from 1 (poor) to 10 (superior), please rate the following elements.

   ____ Heroine   ____ Plot
   ____ Hero   ____ Inspirational theme
   ____ Setting   ____ Secondary characters

5. These characters were special because?_____
_____
_____

6. How has this book inspired your life?_____
_____
_____

7. What settings would you like to see covered in future
   Heartsong Presents books? _____
_____
_____

8. What are some inspirational themes you would like to see
   treated in future books? _____
_____
_____

9. Would you be interested in reading other **Heartsong
   Presents** titles? ❏ Yes ❏ No

10. Please check your age range:
    ❏ Under 18   ❏ 18-24
    ❏ 25-34   ❏ 35-45
    ❏ 46-55   ❏ Over 55

Name_____
Occupation _____
Address _____
City_____ State_____ Zip_____

Texas Charm

4 stories in 1

Love is in the air around Houston as told in four complete novels by DiAnn Mills. Four contemporary Texas women seek life's charm amid some of its deepest pain—such as broken relationships and regrets of the past.

Contemporary, paperback, 480 pages, 5 $^3/_{16}$"x 8"

❤ ❤ ❤ ❤ ❤ ❤ ❤ ❤ ❤ ❤ ❤ ❤ ❤ ❤ ❤ ❤

❤ ❤ ❤ ❤ ❤ ❤ ❤ ❤ ❤ ❤ ❤ ❤ ❤ ❤ ❤ ❤

Presents